THE LONG RED HAIR

AND OTHER SHORT STORIES

Nancy J. Martin

Contents

Author's Notes

Writers are always reminded to listen and take note of conversations that they might hear in a café or on a bus. I've found this to be excellent advice for mining info for future stories. I slightly fictionalized two of this book's stories gathered in that manner, adapting true stories unwitting storytellers shared with me. Each time I heard those stories, I raced home to write them down. Other stories are flash fiction, which I enjoy writing, others are memoir pieces, and I added a couple of essays for good measure.

I am indebted to the many good folks taking part in various writing groups who have included me over many years. We shared our work, listened to others' writing, and offered writing prompt suggestions; some of the fiction stories here originate from these suggestions.

THE LONG
RED HAIR

AND OTHER SHORT STORIES

Swamp Tour

Clouds of warm, dense vapor rising from the swamp were so thick I couldn't see my hand in front of my face. Our beat-up, flat-bottomed boat skimmed along, cutting a trail through the intensely green blanket of plant life covering the water. Everything was greener than the emerald city of Oz.

While strolling along a typically bustling street in New Orleans the previous day, a poster taped up inside a shop window grabbed my attention. It advertised an "Authentic Cajun Swamp Tour." A full-color poster displayed the menacing, bumpy, open jaws of an alligator snapping up at a boat from the water. Intrigued, I immediately bought two tickets.

Setting out from an area near Metairie, we followed signs through funky backwoods guiding us to the gator tour boat ramp. A grisly old fellow greeted us and introduced himself as Capn' Seth. "I been living out here on the swamp all my life and know every square inch of this bayou. Come along with me and I promise you won't be disappointed." Signs hanging from his dilapidated road-side shack told us we would be treated to sightings of "...all manner of wild critters in their native habitat including: Alligators!, wild boar, giant river turtles, bandit-faced raccoons, snakes, owls and many other types of birds." We could hardly wait.

After donning the prerequisite life-vests, Cap'n Seth and his young Cajun helper Joey, who was carrying a rifle ("just in case"), hustled the two of us into their stinky boat. Initially they were both very quiet. The only sounds to be heard in the swamp were the calling of birds and murky water slapping the sides of the boat. As far as the eye could see stood endless groves of ancient cypress trees growing right out of the water. The massive trees creating a canopy in the sky, trailed ribbons of green moss down to float on the surface of the water. Our boat glided along, snaking its way through twists and turns through the overgrown aqueous landscape. We were enchanted with the natural beauty and tranquility of the swamp.

Soon enough Cap'n Seth began to spin out swamp stories. Apparently, keeping pets such as dogs and cats anywhere in this bayou country was a risky business. Alligators were thick as thieves and tended to favor small critters for a quick snack. These fearsome reptiles were not discriminatory. "Folks had best keep a close eye on small children too," as it was not unheard of for alligators to carry them off. And we thought shark attacks back home on the California coast were gruesome.

The damp, hazy mists surrounding our small open boat were becoming thicker and I wondered how we would ever find our way back. We were advised not to dangle our hands outside of the boat. "Pretty soon we'll be thick in alligator territory." Right away I heard loud snapping sounds like breaking glass. Yikes! *Exactly* like the photo on the poster, huge elongated, bumpy green jaws began to surface, threatening to chomp down on the sides of our boat. Cap'n Seth chuckled as he tore open a big bag of fluffy white marshmallows. "Watch this." He lobbed a fat marshmallow covered with powdered sugar right into the hideous open jaws of a huge prehistoric-looking creature looming near the boat. Suddenly the waters all around us were roiling with razor-toothed snapping jaws. Our boat was completely surrounded! Large round protruding eyes skimming the surface of the water watched us closely, as the scary green critters bared rows of long yellow teeth. It was unnerving. In the recesses of my memory I could hear Captain Hook singing in his low mocking voice..."Never smile at a croc-o-dile." But we were not on a ride in Disneyland. This was real! We scooted closer together into the center of the boat and hung on tight.

As mid-day approached, the sun made a hot, red entrance burning off some of the fog. We watched giant turtles lumbering along on the banks of small islands. When the bag of marshmallows was empty and the critters sated with their sugar fix began to settle down, the Cap'n slowly turned the boat around to head back. I had taken enough photos to last a lifetime and my husband said that he could use some lunch. "Well alrighty then" said our buddy Capn' Seth, "Then let's head back to the shack and cook you up some authentic gator burgers! Aren't you glad you came?"

Those Colorful Streets

Shopping at Britex on Post Street in San Francisco was my idea of heaven on earth in 1968. Fabulous combinations of cotton candy pink and bright, bright tangerine, or purple, teal, and lime green prints on fresh bolts of multi-fibered fabrics filled the entire store, roof to basement. Getting down on my knees, digging through oversized cardboard cartons of cool remnants and finding an unexpected great deal was a big part of the fun. I was always on the lookout for fabric remnants covered with huge geometric shapes in bright colors or sleek Asian prints to create huge, fluffy, floor pillows. Those comfy creations sold the minute I left them in the crafts stores or consignment shops, providing me with additional dollars to help make ends meet.

Everything was Carnaby Street style then—colors, fashion, and music. Humming along to *Georgy Girl* playing on the store sound system, I'd browse through the sewing patterns for a perfect little minidress to create from my remnant.

Gleefully toting a stuffed Britex bag, my next stop would always be the dance store nearby where they sold leotards and tights in every bright, primary color. Laying my new fabrics on the counter, I'd choose two or three pair of tights in colors to match. This was my look: Psychedelic patterned minidress, jewel-toned tights, knee-high boots, dangling earrings and handmade strands of love beads. My handcrafted bead necklaces were strung on string, while I sat on the edge of my bed, quaffing cheap Red Mountain wine out of a sticky water glass and listening to the very hip sounds of Thelonious Monk.

Prior to the London Mod look, my wardrobe was simply basic black: Black headband, black turtleneck, black bell-bottoms or a black mini-skirt, black tights, and black boots. As protection from the fog and cold I had a heavy, waterproof navy-blue pea jacket purchased cheaply from the local Army/Navy surplus store. This look plus the fact that I wore no make-up at all, simplified getting dressed in the morning.

At the time I was living in a nine-dollar-a-week bare-bones room with a funky bathroom down the hall (shared with junkies, winos, and lots of Ajax) in a run-down, multistoried hotel above a bar on Grant Avenue. My lumpy single bed sat under a window overlooking the street where I could see, smell and, hear all the action. A distinctive bar odor of booze and cigarettes rising from the raucous establishment below permeated our building.

Because upper Grant Avenue and North Beach were predominantly Italian neighborhoods, that lovely garlicky scent of simmering sauce would come wafting down the street from the Old Spaghetti Factory as soon as they started sautéing the sugo in the morning, enhanced by yeasty mouthwatering aromas from the ovens of various bakeries in the neighborhood. Always there was Italian opera leaking through the walls and windows out on to the street, in competition with Jimmy Hendricks screaming from the kid's rooms.

The neighborhood was a wonder. On my days and nights off I walked the colorful neighborhood streets soaking it all up. Because I was under twenty-one and not yet allowed to purchase alcohol, I would usually end up nursing a cappuccino at Caffe Trieste on the corner of Grant and Vallejo Streets. Often someone would bring bongos offering a beat to the verse — our 1960's rap. Later, filled with inspiration I'd always end up at City Lights Books to spend money I should have saved for food.

Music was my other obsession. There was a great record store on the corner where I also spent money I didn't have. There wasn't much in my room, but I had everything I needed. My portable sewing machine and a record player, both propped up on boxes and a pile of books in the corner filled it up. Classical chamber music would start me off to work in the morning and always jazz at night. I was learning to appreciate rock music, but distained hippies. Although I was too young, in my own opinion I was a member of the beat generation.

Grant Avenue is split down the middle with Italians on one end and Chinatown at the other. My favorite place for cheap eats was a very funky Chinese diner called Fuey Guey Louie's. Perching on a red swivel stool at the counter I could fill up for practically nothing. Since I didn't speak Chinese, I'd just point to a plate that looked good. Best to finish it up as I had no kitchen or even a tiny fridge to store leftovers. Unlike today, there were no homeless people sitting on the curb who would want leftover food.

On sunny days, I'd wander down to Washington Square Park in the heart of Little Italy, across the street from Saints Peter and Paul church, first stopping at Liguria Bakery for a café latte and some cannoli so fresh they would melt on my tongue. Or maybe a hike up Telegraph Hill for a visit to Coit Tower to take in the incredible 360-degree views and brilliantly colored historic wall murals would be just the ticket.

The intersection of Broadway and Columbus near Grant was the "seedy" part of the hood. Barkers stood in the doorways of strip clubs and peepshows, loudly beckoning roving gentlemen to enter and harassing girls on the street. I knew to always watch my back at night. Best to avoid being noticed unless you were in the business of selling sex.

My friend Sally, worked at Joseph Magnin on Stockton and O'Farrell, an upscale fashion emporium selling hip styles, which appealed to us young working girls. With her silky, lustrous hair shimmering almost down to her hips and even longer legs, Sally always looked like she had just stepped out of the store window. Guys were always trying to pick us up—"wanna smoke a joint?"—which we politely declined, not wanting to get busted. Sally was always a hoot and full of good ideas. "How about if we catch a bus on Saturday and ride down to Sausalito to hang out for the day?"

If there were any place I'd ever been that would qualify as the most awesome place on earth, it would be Sausalito. So, when the weekend rolled around, we hopped onto the bus, eagerly anticipating whatever the day might offer.

The bus dropped us off on Bridgeway, Sausalito's picturesque main drag, the entirety of which curved around Richardson Bay. A bright sun sparkled out on the water, wrapping all the sailboats in diamond necklaces and the breeze so fresh it literally smacked me in the face with a big kiss. This was an entirely different world only fifteen minutes out of the city. We made a beeline for The Tides Bookstore. Inside, the old batten and board building was warm and fragrant with its comforting redolence of books, coffee, and donuts.

The Tides always had great music playing and the people-watching was the best. We wandered around taking our time, checking out titles and reading poetry. When each of us had selected something, we met up for a cup of free, strong, hot coffee, settling in some cozy, well-worn chairs in a corner and blissfully whiled away the morning.

Fortified with caffeine, we made our way down the main drag and through the side-streets, meandering in and out of chic shops and jewelry stores. Further down Richardson Street on the bayside was a tiny shop in a beat-up little shack. If you didn't sew or knit you'd probably pass it by, but I always had to go in and check out the handcrafted buttons and other lovely artistic notions which included exquisite ribbon trims which everyone, back in the day, sewed to the hems of their bell-bottoms. These unique little items made a huge fashion statement in the 60's.

Crossing the street Sally and I agreed that we were starving. Soupçon was my favorite place in Sausalito for cheap eats. You could smell the enticing fragrance of the soups long before stepping through the door. Every day the chefs would cook up giant kettles of a few mouthwatering varieties and serve huge, steaming bowls with a hunk of freshly baked sourdough French bread for mopping up the savory goodness. Soup—the ultimate comfort food. It just didn't get any better than that.

Not wanting to miss the sun setting over the city,

we typically made it a point to get back on the bus just before sundown. No matter how many years I had lived in San Francisco, it always blew my mind to cross the Golden Gate Bridge, coming home to a panoramic sunset settling over downtown. From our seats on the bus as it approached the bridge we watched the lights across the bay, illuminating the skyline of downtown high-rises and around the coastline to the Sea Cliff neighborhood, always an unforgettable moment. Hanging out in marvelous Marin was fun, but we loved returning to The City.

Life Review

"Ohhh Mommy, look how cute. I want that one. Please, oh please!" The owners of the parent dogs with their litter of four stood by looking on proudly. "These are prize-winning, pedigreed toy poodles, as advertised. Both parents are champion show dogs. These pups will make excellent pets and companion dogs for children." Six-year-old Cathy was swooning over one of the blond pups. She was lying on the floor and the puppy was bouncing all over her, licking her face. Following some discussion between her parents and the dog breeders, Cathy chose her pup and they left to go home. "Geez, I can't believe we paid that much for *a dog,*" her dad was telling them once they were safely ensconced inside their shiny red SUV. Mom had brought along a pink satin-lined puppy bed. Cathy and the new puppy snoozing in its lavish little bed were in the back seat where Cathy sat watching a video of a dog show on the overhead screen.

"Can we call her Honey? She's almost the color of honey."

"Sure sweetie, that's a cute name. But we'll have to come up with a fancy name for her registration papers. You watch her Cath, make sure she doesn't fall out of her bed."

"Oh Mom, I would *never* let anything happen to Honey. She'll be the number one most pampered dog in the whole world."

Honey began to whine. *"How could they let these people take me away from my brothers and sisters? I want my mom."* Cathy immediately picked up her new puppy and snuggled it against her cheek. "Don't worry little one, you're going to love your new home."

As time went on, it was clear that Honey ruled the roost. Nothing was too good for the little golden poodle. She was Cathy's most cherished possession, companion and family member. Honey had a huge, manicured back yard with a swimming pool as her domain. She was taken regularly to a pricey pet groomer in town and was allowed to sleep with Cathy in her bed. *"Everyone knows that I am a queen. Only the best for me,"* were Honey's ever-present thoughts while snubbing the neighbor's mutt or contentedly snacking on a piece of rare steak. Humility was not her strong suit.

Twelve years went by in a flash. *"How could you leave me here in this dreadful, smelly place in a cage, surrounded by the motley vulgus of the dog world?"* Stuck with needles and force-fed medicine that caused her to vomit, Honey felt herself slipping away.

The first thing he could remember was waking in a cramped cage on a filthy blanket with his mom and many siblings—all different colors. He would have dreams of people petting him and feeding him good food. "Look at these ratty little bastards. They'll bring plenty in the fight ring." The men came twice a day to feed mom and toss them around, often inflicting pain on the little pups. "We gotta make 'em mean from the get-go."

Bruno was ninety pounds of pure muscle and bone. He hated the men. He had long since been separated from his canine family and placed in a small foul cage. Every day one of the men either mercilessly beat him or threw him in with another dog to fight over food, often leaving him wounded. After one year when he reached full weight capacity and knew nothing but to fight for his life, the night arrived when they took him in a truck with other dogs to an unfamiliar place. *"This won't be good,"* the dogs told each other. *"Some of us won't come back."*

The room was thick with smoke and the sounds of snarling dogs. Coarse, angry men shouted out bets and curses. Bruno was chained to the side of a large fight ring at a safe distance from other dogs. He had a pretty good idea what would happen next. Soon enough he heard a man on the loudspeaker say his name. His handler roughly dragged him into the ring where another man on the other side was doing the same with his dog. When a bell rang the handlers released their dogs, who rushed at each other snapping and snarling.

It was kill or be killed. Bruno felt his hide being ripped apart. Tasting blood from his attack on the opposing dog only heightened his hatred and will to live. Soon enough the dogs were separated before one of them died in the ring. Bruno was stitched up in several places and medicated into a deep sleep. Always hungry and in pain, this became the pattern of his life until one of his opponents finally conquered him. But throughout his pitiful life he always dreamed the dream of a pampered life.

It was a typical day at the animal shelter. Approaching the driveway of the facility they could hear the cats and dogs. When James and Martha entered the building, friendly volunteers greeted them and gave them information about dog adoption. A dog section volunteer took over, directing them down the long hallway of cages filled with dogs waiting for a good home. Another welcoming volunteer collected their adoption application, explaining to them how many of the rescued dogs had been mistreated and abused, leaving them wary and shy. Other dogs howled and angrily lunged at the cage doors. Some looked very sad and others were listlessly eating or sleeping.

One of the dogs, a medium-sized black and brown mixed breed with silky ears, quietly approached the front of his cage and seemed to smile at them. Bob asked the volunteer, "What's the story with this dog?"

"This is Quigley, he's a good old boy just looking for his forever home. Somebody picked him up on the street and brought him here, but nobody has ever come looking for him. He's been here for about six months and never given us a bit of trouble."

James and Martha took Quigley to a quiet room in the animal shelter where they could observe him. He lay right down next to James, resting his jaw on James' left sneaker, gazing up at him adoringly with soulful brown eyes. Well that pretty-well clinched the deal, and they left with the dog. They re-named him Buddy. When Martha came home from work every day, Buddy would be over the moon with joy. Her classic comment was, "Dogs are so nonjudgmental, they just want you to love them." James would take Buddy out for walks or to jog with him in the evenings. Folks passing by often stopped to offer Buddy a pat on the head or a scratch behind the ears and often quipped, "That is one happy dog. He is actually smiling!"

Most dogs dream, but Buddy had howling dogmares. When he wasn't dreaming about living a contented life, he would have unbearable visions of beatings and pain. First James would feel his dog begin to tremble, hear the high-pitched whining begin and then notice snapping and growling. Buddy's legs would begin to kick and run in an uncontrollable frenzy.

But always, through the fog and confusion of his dream he would hear James' voice cutting through the mental trauma; "Hey Bud, you're dreaming. Come back." And he would.

My Totem Bear

During our Yosemite road trip, we began discussing bears. "You know," I told my friend who was gazing in wonder at the scenery outside, "You have to be really careful about bears once we get into the valley. Over the years tourists have been careless and now the bears are a big problem."

Despite my many trips to Yosemite Valley, it would be Katie's first time in this amazing place. We pulled into the parking lot of one of the visitor centers and went to the front desk. The very first thing we saw was a monitor on the counter playing a video of an enormous bear smashing a car window and wiggling in to retrieve the remains of a sandwich on the back seat. My friend couldn't believe it. "Whoa, I thought you were exaggerating about the bear problem." We saw signs stating guidelines for avoiding bear encounters. The signs clearly stated that nothing with a food scent, not even a candy wrapper, should be left in a car. Not only that, special anti-bear trash receptacles were everywhere we looked. "Holy cow, you weren't kidding, they're really on the case about bears around here!" Checking in to our room we noticed more anti-bear advisories in the motel lobby.

A few years earlier my friend Joy, the owner of a a remote Canadian fly-fishing lodge, told me many hair-raising stories about her personal bear encounters. She made it clear that you shouldn't ever fool around with a bear of any age. "Baby bears might look cute, but the mother would just as soon eat you as notice you even looking at her baby." Then she gave me a memoir written by a Canadian woman who had been attacked by a bear in the wild. I read the book thinking that it would make for interesting discussion later. However, by the time I turned the last page I was having serious reader regret. The poor author described her bear attack in horrific detail. It chewed off half of her face before sauntering off, leaving her for dead. Following years of repeated plastic surgeries and excruciating pain she had written the memoir.

Prior to the reading of this unfortunate story, I had considered myself mostly free of fear. I had no fear of heights, flying, insects, snakes, the dark or just about anything else. But now I found myself burdened with a deadly fear of bears. Nightmares about giant bears with their long snouts gnawing at my body parts woke me in a sweat. I no longer thought that teddy bears were adorable. When the grammar school where

I happily volunteered with small children needed drivers for a field trip to the teddy bear factory, I declined.

Spending the weekend in Yosemite Valley in close proximity to countless bears was bound to be challenging. "Just follow the rules," I thought, still withholding this phobia from my friend. Later that evening, I suggested going to the Ahwahnee Lodge for a drink. We merrily hopped onto the park shuttle bus. The historic hotel is almost a museum in its own right, adorned throughout with splendid Native American baskets, pottery, photos and rugs hung from the log walls. This was right up Katie's alley. She delighted in every bit of our self-guided tour. Then we went down to the bar where a good-looking man was playing jazz standards on a baby grand for the hotel guests. At the end of his set, Fred the piano player, sat down at our table where we spent the remainder of the evening swapping stories and tipping back a drink or two. The Ahwahnee is famous for its dramatic floor to ceiling windows which provide unparalleled views of the park. As darkness descended, I suggested we catch the last shuttle back to our motel. Fred chuckled, telling us that we had missed our ride an hour before. "But," he told us "it will be a beautiful walk back in the moonlight."

Katie did not think a thing about the prospect of walking back through the dark secluded forest. I finally fessed up as we walked. "Bears," I lamented.

"We'll surely be attacked and eaten by bears!" My friend just laughed at me. "Come on, we're rough and tumble cowgirls. Think of all the scrapes we've been through. You can't really be afraid of bears?" But as soon as we spied a set of headlights approaching, I ran out into the middle of the road waving my arms like a mad person. A carload of park workers pulled over. "What's wrong, do you need help?" When I asked for a ride they motioned around the car, indicating that they were full up and drove off, leaving me and Katie alone on the cold, dark road. Maybe ten minutes later, the headlights of another car approached and I hot-footed it back out onto the roadway. Thankfully, this time it was our old buddy Fred the piano player who opened his door and invited us in. We didn't mention anything about bears.

After that trip I took a lot of ribbing about bears. One day after a typically fabulous day out on the trail, with our mounts safely loaded in the horse trailer, we climbed into the cab of my pickup. Starting up the engine I felt something under my boot. Glancing down I saw a shiny object glinting up at me. Honest to God, it was a good-sized sterling silver pin—an engraved bear. Looking over at Katie and holding up the pin, I thought she was playing a trick on me. But she appeared as amazed as I was and swore up and down that she had never seen the pin before. We were utterly baffled. For weeks after that we tried to sort out every possible scenario that could have brought

the silver bear to my truck. No one ever did claim it
and my totem bear remains to this day pinned to the
lapel of my denim jacket.

More Than Life Itself

Patti was determined to have another baby. Since her divorce from John, she and Ethan, her 3-year-old toddler, lived with her parents in her childhood home. Although she was happy enough sharing a bedroom with Ethan, the desire for another child had finally become undeniable.

Seated at the battered old maple breakfast table in the morning with coffee steaming from her mug, she felt a serious need to express her feelings. "Mom, I've made a decision and I hope you'll understand. Even though I'm not seeing anyone, I really want to have another baby." Looking confused, her mother asked, "Don't you need two people to make a baby?"

"Seriously Mom, I've given this a lot of thought. You know that I'm not dating now and am not into one night stands. This is just for Ethan and me. You and I were both only children. I want Ethan to grow up with a brother or sister."

"So, what's your plan, sweetheart?"

"Mom, I've decided that the best thing to do is go to a sperm bank. It will be simple and there won't be any entanglements with the father."

"Wow! Give me a minute to wrap my head around this concept."

"Honestly mom, I don't mean to be disrespectful, especially since you and Dad do so much for Ethan and me. Please understand that this is something I've been thinking about for a long time. I'd like to do it as soon as possible. Do you think you and Dad could handle having two young kids here?"

Patti's mother, Janet was young when she married. Her husband had come into the marriage with two preschool-aged children. A few years later when they announced their plans about divorce to the children, the kids asked if they could live with their stepmother? Janet was thrilled and her soon-to-be-ex-husband agreed to the plan. She loved and raised them into adulthood as her own.

When Janet remarried to Patti's father Tom, he was already the father of three kids from his previous marriage. All the kids came and went between households during school holidays and summer vacations. Janet and Tom embraced the raising of six children, including Patti, their own daughter, who came last. Now adults, the older children raised families of their own. This explained Janet's surprise when Patti asked about taking care of another child. "You're kidding—right? Your dad and I could not love Ethan more. We would welcome another baby if you feel ready for the responsibility."

Patti went online and reviewed the many fine points and options involved in sperm bank impregnation. Finally, she felt committed and signed an agreement to proceed with the process. She started evaluating different sperm donors to help make a decision. There was seemingly no end to the list. The donors were nameless, listed only by number. Each man was described by hair and eye color, ancestry, height and weight. His bio also included things such as a health history, temperament, education and hobbies along with musical and athletic ability. Patti reviewed the extensive list of traits and kept focusing on the one man who seemed ideal. The donor listed himself as 6 feet tall, with light brown hair and blue eyes like her mother's. His educational achievements were impressive, and he was involved in numerous sporting activities. After spending long hours poring over the donor list, #6300728 sounded like the right father for her child. Finally, she made a firm decision and an appointment at the sperm bank clinic.

Her mom drove her into the city. They were both nervous. "Oh Mom, I'm so excited! This baby will belong to me. I'll never have to worry about divorce or an ugly custody battle like I had with John. When Ethan is older I'll explain how and why I made the decision to give him a sibling and of course I'll be honest with my second child. This little girl or boy will always be sure that they were wanted more than life itself." Nine months later Patti gave birth to Adrian, a perfect and beautiful baby girl with big blue eyes. Gramma Janet and Grampa Tom were thrilled, and Ethan was proud to be a big brother.

Janet was a chronic insomniac who often surfed the web late at night when everyone else was asleep. She had an urge to check out the sperm bank website and discovered that she could input #6300728 and get a read-out. Although the site did not give the donor's name or address, it did offer information about other families who had benefited from his gifts. Janet discovered a lot more than she had anticipated. In fact, #6300728 had fathered quite a few children all over the USA. Patti was listed, along with all the other parents of the father donor's children.

The following morning, Janet contacted the individual at the top of the donor list, located in Ohio. A woman answered who, although taken by surprise, was polite. The mother and Janet had a long conversation and exchanged contact info. Her young son was Adrian's half-brother. Because the call went so well, Janet then contacted parents in New York, Hawaii, Seattle, and Tennessee.

Janet and Tom had a spacious and comfortable RV. They loved packing it up and driving across the country to tour places they had never seen before. Janet made plans to visit the family in Ohio. By the time they left she and Tom had become very friendly with Jamie, Adrian's stepbrother and his parents. After that, the kids exchanged Christmas and birthday gifts and sent photos. Jamie called Janet "Gramma."

Eventually, Janet and Tom paid a visit to each of the homes on #6300728's list and in turn, each of the families eventually came to California to visit Adrian. All of the kids were adorable. Many of them had big blue eyes and all of them now called Janet "Gramma." There were two sets of twins, making a total of seven sperm donor siblings.

The kids all got on FaceTime, sharing the events of their days in school, homework, happy times and problems. They always said how much they loved knowing their half-siblings. Photos were posted on Facebook and Instagram, showing the various kids at birthday parties and holidays. Gramma Janet and Grampa Tom were happily spending a fortune during the holidays on gifts for the many grandchildren. When Adrian was old enough to go to school, she told her mom that when kids asked about her dad, she would tell them that her mom wanted her "more than life itself."

Revisiting the sperm bank website, Janet noted each donor had a specific time frame in which to donate. She saw that there were just 2 more donations available from #6300728. Now her burning question was: would there be 2 more grandchildren yet to come? She could hardly wait to see their adorable little faces.

The Long Red Hair

Rolling along on a Greyhound bus in 1969, watching the unfamiliar passing landscape speed by, I was bound for Fort Lewis after enlisting in the Army. When we came to a lurching stop, a young kid swinging a duffle bag got in and sat down next to me. Turning to look at each other, we each did a double-take. By golly we could have been twins. Back then, I had beautiful auburn hair. Not your everyday flaming, garish red, but thick, lustrous, soft auburn hair, flowing down to my waist. I'll have to admit that I was a bit vain about that hair, investing in pricey shampoo and conditioning products to maintain its beauty like a teenaged girl. It wasn't unusual for young guys like me to have hair down to their shoulders back in the time of long-haired hippies. Girls would go crazy for that hair, always wanting to get their hands into it.

The boy's hair was exactly the same color as mine. He could easily have passed for my kid brother. We shot the bull for a while and I asked him if he'd like to join me for a beer at the next stop. "Oh thanks but I can't. I'm under 21. They won't serve me."

"They will now buddy," I said, handing him my photo ID, telling him to keep it, knowing I wouldn't need it after I got my military ID and they shipped me over to Nam. From the look on his face, I might have just handed him a million bucks!

We really enjoyed sucking down those ice-cold beers at the rest stop. As soon as the bus got underway again, he plunged into a blissful sleep. As we approached his stop, I nudged him awake. He opened his eyes with a sweet smile on his face, pulled his bag out from under the seat and walked to the door of the grimy bus, across from our driver who was cranking open the squeaky door to let him out. Turning back to me, the kid raised his hand in a cheery wave goodbye, then spread the first and second fingers of his hand in a peace sign and exited the bus, gleefully in possession of his brand-new photo Id. Knowing that my tour of duty would begin right away, I doubted I'd see my new little bro again. But he had my id and address. I hoped he'd write.

Because I'd enlisted, I wasn't scared or worried. My older brother was a Navy SEAL and had filled me in on what to do and should expect at bootcamp. Miles into my bus journey, a well-dressed woman boarded the bus, took the empty seat beside me, and we chatted. Right away she commented on my hair, admiring my wavy auburn tresses. Recounting my enlistment story, I told her, "So when I get to Fort Lewis they'll cut it all off." She looked horrified. "No, they won't! *Please let me do it.* I'll give you five hundred dollars for that luxurious head of hair. I'm a hairdresser. I could have three wigs made from all of that." I got off with her at the next stop in a quaint little berg. We walked down the block and entered Lucy's Locks, her salon. Sitting myself down in one of her hairdressing chairs, I felt somewhat sheepish. She threw a cape over me and, snipping away, cut my hair really short—carefully hoarding every single hair— then shaved my head. I left five hundred bucks richer. Plus, an extra bonus! The nice lady called a cab and paid the driver to take me to the Fort.

Arriving at the base, my smooth, gleaming pate shining in the sun, I cracked up when they sent me off with everybody else to get a haircut. Laughing, I told my Sargent, "Ya gotta be kidding Sarge, I'm bald."

"*Everybody* goes and no backtalk from you private! **Get in line.**"

After we marched to the barbering station, a soldier instructed me to sit down. A mean-looking guy with huge shears asked me, "How do you want it?" I couldn't believe it. "Really? I'm already bald."

"EVERY SOLDIER GETS A CUT" and he proceeded to shave my already bald head, yet again.

Ruby's Revenge

I received a road trip invitation to Colorado from my horseback riding buddy, Christine, to visit our friends Larry and Dana. This couple were outfitters who took visiting hunters up into the Rockies on horseback to hunt for elk and owned a sprawling, picturesque ranch in the mountains that was also a cowboy bed and breakfast.

Passing through Nevada and Utah, we stopped for a night to get some rest and a hot meal. Enjoying the changing scenery and finally arriving in Colorado, we passed Denver and made a lunch stop in the charming skiing village of Vail.

Driving through Glenwood Springs on the way up to Carbondale, Christine regaled me with the history of the ranch. The extensive one hundred and eighty-five acres of ranch lands had been in Larry's family since the 1970s. The property, located in the exquisite and pristine upper Crystal River Valley, is surrounded by the White River National Forest. She explained that the Crystal River remains one of the last free-flowing rivers in the west. The ranch property, nestled at the base of Saddle Mountain, boasts views from every angle that go on as far as the eye can see. A good-sized river runs right through the ranch. The dramatic scenery etched my first impressions of the ranch into my memory as we drove in.

Huge racks of elk antlers, serving as chandeliers, coat and hat racks, and pot hangers, adorned the spacious B&B. In their kitchen, the large commercial freezer was well stocked with various cuts of elk meat, which the couple and their hands had hunted, butchered and packaged. Every evening, Dana would cook up big family-style dinners for their guests, shared in the rustic dining room, warmed by a fire in the huge handcrafted, stone fireplace. Larry built the inn and it is the real deal. If you hankered for the cowboy lifestyle, this was the place to be.

After a good night's sleep, we had considerable work to do before the next group of guests arrived. We knew they would be eagerly anticipating their rocky mountain experience, guided by actual Colorado cowboys. On a sparkling, clear morning, we went down to the barn with Larry and his wrangler. Our job that day would begin by riding to the upper pastures, to bring down a loose herd of horses. As we rounded up the herd, a pretty, young chestnut mare captured my attention. I asked Larry if I could ride her later when we took the tourists out and I clearly remember his answer on that fateful morning. "You want to ride Ruby today? Well sure, why not?"

After brushing down the horses, we went back across the river and down to the house to share one of Dana's mouthwatering breakfasts with the guests. It was still early when we rode out with the hunting party. Larry had grown up on the ranch and knew his way around those mountain elk trails like nobody's business. Riding straight up through the aspens was quite a sight. They didn't name those mountains "The Rockies" for nothing. Our sturdy mounts carried us over boulders and beds of slate. All the while, Larry pointed out interesting pieces of information. "See all the scarring on the aspens? That bark contains a natural form of aspirin. When the elk are freezing and starving because their food is under the snow, they gnaw on those trees to give themselves some relief."

I had been riding drag on Ruby all day, bringing up the rear. Earlier, when the horses were still fresh, Ruby began acting up, giving me a good round of bucking and the wrangler said, "You sat that buck real good!" By late afternoon, we had been in the saddle for over four hours and the horses were showing signs of fatigue. No one had yet bagged an elk. It was cold and my feet were getting numb. To get some relief, I took my feet out of the stirrups and let my legs hang loose, thinking that the horse would be too tired to fret. Then in the cooling evening air, reaching behind me to untie my jacket from the saddle, I slipped my right arm down into a sleeve. The left arm went down next and then shot straight out as I shimmied into the coat. But at that very second, when I was most vulnerable, with no hands or feet to steady me, that dang horse began to buck like crazy. She had caught my sudden action out of the corner of her eye. Instinctively grabbing for the saddle horn, I sat out a few bucks, but with no feet in the stirrups I was a dead duck. Later, Larry said the horse had been rarely ridden and never trained. He figured that by the time I was through with her, she would be safe to ride.

My final memory is of soaring through the air. Fortunately, I was wearing a riding helmet, for which I had taken unmerciful grief and teasing from the men all day. But when I came to, everyone said, "Oh thank God you were wearing a helmet." That horse had thrown me quite a distance, right into a big pile of stones. I heard Ruby had turned around and came back at the gallop to attack me on the ground. Though I was in shock, I knew I was injured but couldn't pinpoint the specific injury. That night I heard someone say that all the riders circled around to protect me from the crazy horse.

We were still two hours away from the ranch by horse. So Larry took one of the hunters off of reliable old Gus, helping the man up onto his own horse. They boosted me up onto Gus and Larry got onto Ruby, then proceeded to beat the daylights out of her. After riding down the mountain for a while, we came to a deserted line cabin. Christine asked if I'd like to get off and rest? We were both surprised when I said "yes." In all the many hours we'd ridden together, I'd never wanted to get off of my horse. When we got back on the horses, I turned to Christine and asked her, "By the way, where are we staying tonight?" My answer terrified her. Where else would we be staying? She announced to the group, "We need to get this one to the hospital right away."

After spending the night in the hospital—packed in ice—watching the snow falling outside my window was purely ironic. The next day, Christine got me onto a plane. Despite my pain, I remained unaware that the Glenwood Springs hospital had missed diagnosing my badly broken clavicle. Back in Santa Rosa, an x-ray finally revealed the break, and I was sent home with my arm in a sling.

But here's the kicker: Some months later when our friends brought a stock trailer full of horses from Colorado to California, to winter over, we all went out for a ride. That day, Larry was riding Ruby. All was calm and peaceful as we rode around the lake at Christine's ranch. Suddenly, without warning, Ruby began to buck hard, sending Larry flying, barely missing a pile of rusty barbed wire. He was really ticked off! Then he re-mounted and once again proceeded to kick her butt. Later they called from Colorado to tell us that crazy Ruby had even tossed off their head horse wrangler. Justice was served when they sold that nasty mare to a rodeo to perform in the bucking string. Just goes to show that looks aren't everything.

Rumors

Could it be true? Surfing through Facebook, I had noticed my friend Ann's name pop up. There was a picture of Ann standing very close to a man that was *not* her husband Garrett. I knew that the photo could have been snapped anywhere and might be completely innocent. I couldn't believe she would cheat on him. But the more I thought about it, the more I wanted to know who the heck that man was. It would be rude to call Ann and ask. The photo was out there on the web and once rumors started, they had a tendency to snowball. I had to find out.

Finally texting Ann, we made a lunch date for the next day, meeting at one of our favorite cafés. Sitting outdoors on the patio shaded by large striped umbrellas, I waited for my friend to arrive. Mature plantings of trees and colorful pots filled with fragrant flowers provided privacy between the tables. Uncharacteristically nervous, I was not sure how to begin. When Ann arrived we met with our usual hug and sat down to peruse the menu. Settling in with customary glasses of cold white wine, we chatted about everyday things. Trying to keep my cool I finally asked Ann "What's new?"

"Oh, I'm so excited," she told me, "My husband is absolutely the greatest! Garrett is so romantic, he's taking me to Hawaii for our anniversary." I had to admit to myself that I was jealous and waited for the bombshell, but she only talked about work and family, never mentioning another man in her life. I just couldn't bring myself to ask about the man in the photo. Following a pleasant lunch we went on our separate ways.

Soon, inevitable gossip began to spread. Chloe called. "I saw a man in a photo with Ann on Facebook. What a hunk. Is he Ann's boyfriend? Is she cheating on Garrett?" Doing my best to dispel any potential malice, I made light of Chloe's suggestion and got right off the phone. My mind was really buzzing now. The not knowing kept me awake all night.

The next afternoon, huddled discreetly in my car I waited for Ann to emerge from the office building where she worked and drive off in her car. Feeling guilty-as- hell, I began to follow her from a distance so I wouldn't be spotted. But she only went to the grocery store and then straight home. I was consumed with the notion that Ann was cheating on Garrett and began to spend more time stalking her. Devising devious plans to track Ann's movements and following them out, I was never able to discover her doing anything out of the ordinary. The obsession to catch my friend in some perverse behavior began to take over my life. Not sleeping or feeling like eating, I began to drink more than I should and spend way too much time pouring over social media sites. I even stopped going to the gym.

One afternoon, while sitting in my car, the man in the photo came out of Ann's office building. Double-checking the Facebook photo on my phone I could see that it was *him*. My mind was in a frenzy, sure now that I would eventually find the two of them together. Day after day I waited, following Ann in hopes of discovering something—anything. I *needed* to catch them.

Slumped behind the wheel of my car at the end of office hours I watched the mystery man leaving the office building. Finally coming to the realization that I wasn't getting anywhere tracking Ann, I decided to start stalking the man in the photo. Turning, he began walking down the block. I quickly took the initiative to follow him on foot, careful to keep my distance. He didn't know me so I was not worried about being spotted. After walking a few blocks, he stopped to enter a bar. Peering through huge windows on the street I could see that the place was packed. Stepping in through the front door, the sound of loud music assaulted my senses. People were three-deep at the bar and tables were full. Attempting to scan the scene, I looked for the man in the photo. He was hanging out at the bar chatting with another guy. Snaking my way through the shifting crowd, I managed to sidle up into a position with my back turned to the man. Stepping back, I bumped into him. Spinning around to face him, I managed to flash my most beguiling smile. "Oh gosh, I'm so sorry. Did you spill your drink? Please let me buy you another. I'm so clumsy."

Making eye contact, the impact of his dark good looks astonished me. Laughing he mopped the front of his shirt with a cocktail napkin telling me, "It's OK, at least it's the end of the day" and offered to buy me a drink, while ordering another for himself. Feigning embarrassment I accepted the drink. We found an empty 2-top and sat down. "My name's Steve. I'm a department manager at Halo Software a few blocks away. How about you?" After introducing myself and summoning up my courage I asked if he knew my friend Ann who worked there. "Oh yeah. I met her at an office party. She works on my floor." Not discerning any sense of personal connection, I let it go. After a few drinks and a lot of laughs, I said I had to leave. We exchanged business cards and Steve asked, "Would it be ok if I called you?"

A few weeks later, I went to the secluded place in the park and waited. Watching his familiar form coming toward me on the footpath, I felt an overpowering sense of relief. Jumping up from the park bench, I threw my arms around him in a big hug. Instead of our usual passionate kiss, I held him at arm's length by the shoulders. Looking straight into his eyes I blurted, "I hope you'll understand Garrett. I'm so sorry, I never meant to hurt you, but I've met someone else."

Disbelief

Standing in the tepid Tahitian surf, silky fish brushing against my bare ankles caused me to look down through the perfectly transparent water. All the colors of the rainbow reflected up from the myriad of glowing tropical fishes. Moorea was very sparsely populated in 1987, without even one high-rise building yet constructed on the island. Club Med, with cozy grass huts serving as guestrooms, was the only tourist destination. The lovely native Tahitian women—reminiscent of a Gauguin painting—with fragrant flowers laced in their hair, along with most of the very chic European women, wore only sarongs or bikini bottoms, baring their tanned breasts to the sun.

Following a breakfast of fresh tropical fruit and a glorious morning of snorkeling, I opted to take a water aerobics class in the gentle surf and afterward was ready for a nap. Feeling perfectly at ease in a partial state of undress, I lay supine with feet in the water and my bare spine supported by the velvety black sand. Dozing in and out of consciousness without a care in the world was sublime.

Observing hulking Tahitian men paddling dugout canoes along the shoreline, I asked one if he would ferry me across a narrow channel to a tiny adjacent island. On the way across the channel, with my hand lazily skimming through the water alongside the canoe, I was slightly alarmed when looking down, noticed that my ring was gone. My daughter had recently made me a gift of a handsome sterling silver ring, inset with a piece of indigo blue lapis lazuli.

The canoe man dropped me on the island shore-line, where I was the only person in sight. Sitting on the edge of the beach I was daydreaming, with no agenda and nowhere to go. Then, gazing down into the lapping crystal clear water, I saw a sparkle of silver and watched in amazement, as my ring washed up between my feet.

Where's The Fire?

It was the only school of its kind in our well-heeled Northern California community. I was a long-term volunteer there and loved every minute of it. The independent K-6 elementary school in the downtown section of our city was located just a few blocks from a large well organized homeless shelter. Historically, this facility cared for a large population of drug and alcohol abusers, many with young children.

The school's charter focused on providing an education for at-risk kids. When families checked in, the shelter would recommend that the children be enrolled at our school. The school recommended that the parents take parenting classes, and required them to volunteer once a week in their kid's classrooms. We got familiar with the various family dynamics very quickly.

Because we loved working with children, a large group of us volunteered. I was a "roving" volunteer, pitching in wherever I was needed. You might find me chopping veggies in the kitchen, doing yard duty at recess, helping with the after-school homework program or assisting as a teacher's aide. The school ran financially by the seat of its pants, providing four free meals each day including a hot breakfast and lunch along with midday and after-school snacks with generous assistance from the local food bank.

Often these kids would arrive at school with an empty stomach. The morning one little boy told me he was hungry because, "My dad shoots all our food money into his arm," I cooked him up a bowl of oatmeal ASAP. At more traditional schools, the first day of school will find many of the students dressed in brand-new outfits. Our kids would arrive rumpled and unclean, sometimes barefoot, so we had a room full of donated clothes. It was fun to take the students in to pick out a new outfit. This would boost their self-esteem and allow them to perform better in the classroom.

One day a fourth-grade girl named Cheryl showed up at school in high heels. Her mom was a streetwalker and would use Cheryl as bait to attract customers. Naturally, Cheryl thought that she looked cool and grown up in the heels until her teacher had a little talk with her. Ms. Connors, the school director had to contact the mother and ask her to "please bring Sheryl to school in more sensible shoes." It would be unusual for a day to pass without having to deal with this kind of inappropriate behavior. Ms. Connors spent a considerable amount of time on the phone conferring with Child Protective Services.

I was out in the schoolyard one sunny day doing yard duty during recess. Kids were lined up waiting to shoot baskets, pummeling a tether ball or hanging out inside the cute, little playhouse making mud pies. I happened to be standing with Ms. Connors alongside the four-square court when a boy named Jimmy slammed the ball over to Gary, a third grader with tousled blond hair, wearing glasses, causing Gary's return shot to go "out" over the line. Gary was the kid who was always in trouble. Hot-headed little Gary hollered at Jimmy telling him, "I'm going to kill you!" I watched Ms. Connors quietly heading in the direction of her office.

A few minutes later a black patrol car and a huge, shiny red fire truck pulled up to the curb right outside of the 8-foot chain-link fence that enclosed the school yard and surrounded the entire school. A city cop emerged from his cruiser and entered the schoolyard gate, followed by a fireman decked out in full firefighter regalia. The kids went bonkers, yelling "Fireman, Fireman," while the teachers and volunteers appearing very alarmed were all asking, "Where's the fire?" My first thought was, "It's this little dude standing right next to me."

By this time, Ms. Connors had returned. She waited calmly as the patrolman approached. He said, "I understand that someone just made a death threat here." Gary's eyes almost popped out of his head. Ms. Connors calmly pointed at Gary. The cop told Gary that making a death threat was a felony offense, punishable by law. Then he asked, "Well I guess I should take him down to the station and book him?" Gary peed his pants right there on the 4-square court, standing paralyzed with fear in his pee-soaked, black and white checkerboard Vans.

A long look was exchanged by Ms. Connors and the patrolman. She took her time answering and then told him, in her calm schoolteacher voice, "No I don't think so. Gary, why don't you come with me to the office so we can call your dad to come and get you. That's probably going to be punishment enough— right?" Following Ms. Connors, Little Tough Guy Gary cried really, really, hard all the way to the school office.

Mediterranean Mishap

In the fall of 2005 our calendar included a date on a Mediterranean cruise ship scheduled to dock in Barcelona, Spain. It was common for us to travel for the winery during much of each year to promote our California wines in the US and abroad. Arriving in Madrid in September, we sweated through a few almost unbearably scorching hot days, the extreme heat foiling our plans to explore the historic capital city of Spain. Staying indoors, we went out only in the evenings for tapas and entertainment. When the sun went down offering more moderate temperatures, the population came out, bringing their children to play in the lovely city parks under a huge Spanish moon.

A few days later we rented a car and made our way from Madrid back to the architecturally renowned and much cooler port city of Barcelona, down to the docks where our multistoried cruise ship was waiting. This excursion turned out to be a big mix-up from start to finish. When we boarded, the cruise line did not have either the winery or my husband's name listed on their schedule as a wine presenter. Later, when they finally took us to a conference room where we viewed myriad bottles of wine on display, we learned that only very few bottles of the wines we were representing had been delivered to the ship. Someone had not followed through and my husband was both embarrassed and infuriated. We sincerely regretted our decision to participate on the cruise. Despite initial concerns, our Mediterranean cruise was comfortable and the winemaker presentation was successful. The weather was glorious, and we signed up for various fun and interesting excursions, dining and shopping at ports along the way in France and Spain.

When our ship returned to the port of Barcelona, we disembarked with absolutely no plans for the remainder of our stay. Inquiring about local day trips at the car rental kiosk, we learned that the favored tourist destination would be a stop at Gibraltar, located at the southern end of the Iberian Peninsula, where many travelers went for nightlife and the social scene. The opposite direction along the Costa Brava, ultimately led to the French border.

Deciding to wander the more serene Costa Brava route we hugged the coast road passing through numerous small, quaint Spanish towns and villages. A tiny, rustic fisherman's café lured us in with the delicious aroma of sardines, freshly pulled from the sea and grilled over an open wood fire. We would remember this simple, delectable meal for years to come. Having no idea, and not really caring where we were going or would end up, I suggested we continue to follow the coastline.

Immediately upon entering the delightfully picturesque village of Tossa de Mar, we instinctively knew that this was where we wanted to stop for the night. Entering a modest hotel that looked promising, we secured a room and for the next few days thought we had died and gone to heaven. On cool and peaceful mornings I spent hours walking in the Old Town exploring the village on my own, navigating a maze of ancient cobblestone streets. Hanging above charming shops offering brightly colored wares of every imaginable variety, a profusion of lipstick-red geraniums spilling out of hand-painted flower boxes adorned apartments topping the old stone buildings. Each day we watched men and women scrubbing down their sidewalks, windows, walkways and storefronts until they sparkled. Our small hotel was immaculate, the weather was balmy and the Spanish food—divine.

This was undoubtedly the friendliest country we had yet visited. Both the local people and tourists we encountered were welcoming and eager to chat. Sharing metal tables on the street with interesting people from all over the world, we drank cappuccino and ate freshly baked mollete bread (think tender English muffins) drizzled with local olive oil and topped with lightly salted, locally grown sliced tomatoes, sweet as sugar. Staying on for a few extra days, we were reluctant to leave this charming village. When finally deciding to depart, we continued on to follow the exquisite coastline of the Costa Brava. This northeastern stretch of the Mediterranean is unparalleled in its natural beauty, a constant irresistible photo op. The colors of the foaming sea crashing against jagged cliffs ranged in vivid shades of aquamarine and topaz to the deepest cobalt blues: with water so clear and pure that when standing on a cliff looking down, the ocean floor was visible. Behind us, The Pyrenees towered majestically between Spain and France. Framed between the mountains and the ocean, the awesome beauty of Catalonia took our breath away. We were enchanted.

Nearing the French border, we reversed direction and drove back to meet our flight home to San Francisco, scheduled to fly out of an airport near Gibraltar. With my husband leading the way, we passed through the scanning device placing our shoes, passports and the contents of pockets, etc., on the belt, which rolled to the other side. When I went through and collected my things, it was apparent that my passport was not in the tray. I searched for my husband but he was nowhere in sight. He had hurried off to the terminal, leaving me to fend for myself although he spoke fluent Spanish and I did not. Attempting to communicate with the evasive customs people was fruitless. Quite shaken, I finally found a kind lady behind a help counter who spoke both English and Spanish. Sensing my near panic, she returned with me to the customs point. Questioning the officials there she determined that one of them did indeed have my passport. She thought that perhaps the man had intended to steal it and then resell it. Then this helpful woman quickly guided me to the correct terminal where our plane was already entirely boarded, waiting for me *with the engines running*. Rushing on to the plane, I saw my thoughtless husband seated and laughing hysterically at my obvious distress. No one else on the plane was laughing. He had been ready to fly off, leaving me alone, unable to communicate and without a passport in a foreign country.

Polarity

It was often difficult to get a straight answer from Lily. No sooner would she express an opinion — sometimes a strong one — then an opposing statement would come right out of her mouth in almost the same breath. Some folks found this amusing. Others were downright put off by her obvious contradictory tendencies. I'd heard people muttering under their breath things like, "How could you ever trust anything she says?"

Although she never admitted it, Lily could not bear to think that someone might not like her. When she was in a Republican crowd, she was a Republican. Conversely, if she was hanging out with Democrats, she would side with their opinions. It was the same story with religion. One day she would devoutly espouse Catholic rhetoric to a person who followed that religion and then claim to be a born-again Christian the following week. This was very confusing for people who knew her. Was she lying? Kissing ass?

Who knew? Did she even know herself? I doubted it.

Early on in our relationship, I noticed she had a big problem with telling the truth. Lily changed her stories to suit the situation so often that it seemed she didn't *really* know what was true or not. Could I trust her? We had been friends for a long time and she was a very charming person. When meeting new people for the first time, her outgoing, glib personality attracted them. She was pretty, flirtatious, wore fashionable clothing and had no trouble attracting men. However, maintaining a romantic relationship was an entirely different matter. Her suitors would soon notice that something was just not quite right and — poof — disappear from her life.

This pattern would send her spiraling down the rabbit hole into deep depressions that might last for weeks. Then she would bounce back up into an irrepressible high. She had no emotional gray areas and was either flying high or very low. Rarely was she simply relaxed. Lily was an emotionally high maintenance friend, but somehow I always felt that she was worth it.

The astrological sign governing her life was Gemini the twins and Lily identified closely with the duality associated with her sign. She had a Gemini key fob, tee shirt, a twins sticker on her car and was often heard to proclaim "I'm a proud and open-minded Gemini." You just had to love her.

I noticed her medication sitting on the sink one

day when I was visiting at her apartment and remembered the name of the drug. A quick Google search revealed its prescription for bipolar syndrome. Then everything became clear to me. I could tell when she was taking her medication or not. The website said that people with this disorder often discontinued the use of their meds because they missed the high, highs. The depression part was obvious.

One morning, while hunkered down in our favorite coffee hangout and reading the newspaper, her life took an upward turn. Seeing an ad offering try-outs for a local theater production, she told me, "Nothing ventured-nothing gained." After that, everything in her life changed forever. A born actress, Lily could move seamlessly from one character or accent to another and no one thought it was weird ever again. She blossomed like a summer rose.

Greg, her current leading man, was instantly smitten with her and soon proposed. One year later Lily and Greg became parents. And wouldn't you know it—they had Gemini twins. A girl and a boy.

The Crux Of Our Guilt

More than ever, many Americans seem to be confused about the differences between right and wrong. A media-driven society presents each of us with skewed and conflicting messages daily. How many of us, while surfing the net, have had a message flashed on our screen about "which foods to avoid ...." One year a prestigious publication will announce that eggs or coffee or meat or grains or wine, etc. are hazardous to our health. Months later, research will claim that a food previously deemed unhealthy is actually good for us. These studies likely included only a few persons and had little or no clinical or scientific backup. Yet we are inclined to believe what we read and haphazardly make changes in our lifestyles to accommodate those beliefs. Popular magazines extensively covered these issues before the internet existed. I hardly recall a time when this informational paradox wasn't public knowledge. Many people are consumed with guilt whenever they eat—or don't eat. What if they are eating the wrong thing, or at the wrong time? They feel the need to discuss these issues during meals with friends and family, often leaving the other person(s) feeling guilty about what is on their plate. This is not good for the digestion.

What about the current craze in counting one's steps? Small fitness devices sell like hotcakes. Merely looking down at our wrist will determine our current fitness level. We can brag to our friends at any moment of the day about how far we've walked, how many steps we have climbed, or how high we've raised our heart rate. Conversely, failure to achieve current fitness goals leaves us feeling guilty. Do we really need to be constantly confronted with this information by attaching a monitor to our body?

These days with fires raging everywhere, people are angry. Their homes and lifelong possessions have gone up in smoke. There must be someone to blame! It must be someone's fault! The utility companies are often to blame, but we forget their workers, who have come out in the dead of night during hideous storms to restore our power and save the melting groceries in our freezers. We also seem to have forgotten Mother Nature's wrath and her destructive ways. All of the fear and subsequent anger leaves us feeling guilty because we don't really know who to blame.

Parenting is always an interesting topic, rife with plenty of reasons for guilt. We all know that babies do not come with instruction manuals and so throughout history, most parents have just done their instinctual best. Sure, lots of parents mess up. But most parents strive to be the best parents they can be. Yet when kids grow up they often fault their parents for their problems. This, of course leads to intensive guilt both on the part of the parents and their children. Finger pointing never pays off.

How about sex? Could there be a more explosive topic centering on guilt? On the topic of oral sex; a man I knew once told me that only whores would do it. His parents had shared that piece of information with him, leaving him with a less than adequate sex life. Almost anything sexual you could think up has been associated with guilt. Let's see: adultery, coveting someone else's spouse, lust, touching (even yourself), not to mention even thinking about sex is considered sinful in some religions. Sometimes not feeling guilty about doing these things is likely to lead to horrendous guilt. Why even bother—knowing you'll end up racked with guilt? Talk about taking all the fun out of playing around.

Pick out any of the "seven deadly sins" and you'll have major fodder for guilt. Who doesn't get angry? Don't we have a right to express our feelings? Granted, letting it go too far is not a good thing. Stepping over the line and murdering someone because they might have a different opinion or killing another motorist during an episode of road rage would be real cause for guilt. Spanking a child used to be the norm. Now it could send you to to prison and you could have double guilt. "Teacher hit me with a ruler"—absolutely no good. Back in the day, if you went home and complained to your parents, they would abuse you for being a troublemaker in school. Three-way guilt! This guilty cycle continues to leak through ongoing generations. The bottom line seems to reveal our entire society. Guilt-ridden to the max with no end in sight.

Never Assume

I was more than a bit surprised when she sat down with me in the break room. We work for a good-sized company and were all hired based on our various skills, both technical and intellectual. Being the boss's personal secretary is a job I love.

Sharon had never really made eye contact with me before. But today, we spent the entire lunch hour snacking and chatting like magpies. While I ate my sandwich and chips, she picked at her plain yogurt and fruit. At the end of our break, we had become better acquainted. When she asked if I'd like to stop for a drink after work, I was pleasantly surprised,

At the end of the workday when I got there, she had already arrived and saved a table at a local watering hole in the downtown neighborhood where people met after work to unwind. The atmosphere was lively and noisy. A group of guys were making a racket, slapping a dice cup down on the bar. Laughing, we almost needed to shout out our requests for drinks and dinner.

When her order of asparagus spears and cauliflower puree was served, she stared at my sizzling burger and fries. The drinks were served, and we chatted as best we could over the noise. After a few drinks, Sharon began asking me a lot of questions about work, but I didn't give it much thought. I had nothing to hide.

She told me that quite a few ladies on our floor went to the same hot yoga class nearby and asked me if I thought I'd be interested in joining them? I'd seen these classes through a window on the street. The very idea of tying myself up in knots while sweating buckets onto my yoga mat, almost triggered a gagging reflex. I politely declined, telling Sharon that I belonged to a local gym and worked out there a few days each week.

On Monday, when the entire group met for midday lunch, I noticed that many of them looked very much alike in a rather eerie manner. They were all bone thin and their hairstyles were similar. Later when they stood up to go back to their cubicles, I noticed that their shoes looked alike too. During lunch they talked continuously about their gluten-free or vegan diets, what they could or couldn't eat and their lunches reflected those preferences. They were chatty, yet vague with me, not exactly friendly, but not unfriendly either. Later, I wondered how I would fit in with them, but was much too busy during my workday to give it any serious thought.

My boss James gave me a lot of leeway in the various capacities of my job. He was fair and even-tempered, never pushing any boundaries or making me uncomfortable in any way. He often talked about his beautiful wife, whose photo with their kids sat on his desk. There was a new baby and an adorable toddler who he was just crazy about. On special occasions he had me send flowers to his wife and seemed very contented with his life.

For a while, I ignored Sharon's subtle hints about her attraction to James. During the times that she suggested we meet, her questions about James just kept coming. Was he happily married? His wife must be a bitch— right? Babies—ugh! Finally, feeling sorry for her, I laid it on the line. He was a very happily married man who would never cheat on his wife.

After that, Sharon wouldn't give me the time of day. When I passed her cubicle and smiled trying to catch her eye, she completely ignored me, along with any emails or texts I sent to her. All of her girlfriends acted exactly the same way, snubbing me in the ladies room or anywhere else I might run into one of them. I'll have to admit that my feelings were hurt. I had stupidly assumed that she liked me as a person and honestly wanted to be my friend. But it was clear that she had just used me as a way to get information about my boss.

When I finally confronted her in the friendliest

possible manner, she acted like I must have imagined the whole thing, now denying any interest in James. I attempted to set up another time for us to meet for drinks, but she claimed to have a very full calendar. I was mystified and felt quite foolish. Never assume.

Slanting Rain

Gloomy winter day or not, I longed to be out on the trail with my horse. It had been raining on and off for days and there would be no way to guess what the weather would be like up on the mountain. Dressing in layers, starting from the skin out with silk long johns and finishing with a fleece throat gaiter I'd be warm as toast no matter what.

Tying a voluminous, rainproof slicker onto the back of my saddle and tucking a sandwich, thermos of steaming hot tea and a few cookies into the saddlebag, The truck had plenty of gas and we were ready to go.

We were both familiar with this park and its interesting variety of trails. Milagro strutted his stuff, more than willing to take me wherever I wanted to go. Being out in the wilderness on my horse was having a reliably blissful effect on my typically stressed-out demeanor. Heaving a huge sigh and deeply inhaling the crisp, clean scent of the forest, I could feel my emotional, spiritual and physical self gradually letting go, as we quietly wended our way up the mountain. We watched tan does guiding their dappled fawns under protective brush and wild turkeys taking clumsy flight up into redwood trees to roost. Jackrabbits with long, black-tipped, translucent ears raced around aimlessly, as we paused to view a hovering, jewel-toned hummingbird drawing nectar from the bell of a wild penstemon blossom the color of cotton candy and saw signs of bobcat scat on the earth below. Luckily, the rattlesnakes were coiled up somewhere under warm rocks and left us alone. This freedom was my most precious treasure. The top of a mountain—my church.

After a comforting stop for lunch and a cup of hot, creamy tea, the sky began to look very threatening, so I slid on my forest green slicker. Then, sure enough, rain began to pour down in buckets. Even though we were still more than an hour away from my rig, I was warm and dry and neither of us felt particularly concerned with the inclement weather.

At the halfway point in our excursion, the wind came up and began to whistle through the towering old growth trees. While horses appear to be impervious to many elements, in my experience they are not fond of wind. Fortunately, equines were created with the uncanny ability to swivel their ears around 180 degrees. This handy little trick allows them to listen closely in any direction. Horses, much like deer, are fight-or-flight animals, using their sharp hearing to aid them in fleeing from danger. The swiveling ears also allow their good-sized ear opening to turn its back on the wind. I noticed Milagro's gracefully pointed, copper-colored ears turn in reverse, to avoid the now-slanting rain, driven by intense winds. Stoically he walked on, sure-footed through the mud. Never one to complain, he trusted that I would guide him back to safety and I in return, placed my trust in him to do the same for me.

Eventually we came around to Two Quarry trail, leading down to the base of the park. Safely returning to the parking lot, I noticed ours appeared to be the only vehicles remaining. Milagro, back in his trailer was contentedly tucking into a bag of fragrant oat hay and a few crunchy carrots, while I covered him with a warm fleece blanket. Climbing up into the cab of my pickup, I had a last sip of the cold, morning coffee remaining in my mug and headed for home.

If The Walls Had Ears

The old house, which stood on a shady, tree-lined street, had been home to the women's club for the last 100 years. With elbows propped firmly behind her on the worn, old Formica countertop, Dana leaned back, eager to hear what her friend had to say. A scant few feet across the familiar little kitchen, Gail—munching contentedly on a cookie—finally began to spill her story. "OK. How do you think the board will react, when I make a motion to donate all the proceeds from our next event to the homeless shelter?"

"Yikes Gail! You know that money was already earmarked to go elsewhere at the last board meeting. Susan will totally come unglued and make an awful scene."

"I know. But in all fairness, she's having a tough time in her life right now. How would you feel if your teenaged daughter was pregnant with the yard guy and dropped out of school? Now he's living there and not even taking care of the yard. All they do is eat and watch TV"

"We'll have to watch out for Gladys too. You know she has issues with homeless people."

"Yeah, she's a spoiled princess who's had a charmed life. Gladys wouldn't recognize want or need if it spit right in her face."

"By the way, let's not forget to make sure that someone stops by to look in on Evelyn. Those chemo treatments have been hard on her, since they removed her breast and her no-good husband dumped her. She might need help with rides to the doctor too."

Dana took a deep breath. Looking around the quaint little room she had a sudden realization. "Imagine all the stories that have been told over the years in this kitchen? Jeez, if the walls had ears."

Caravan

Looking back after all the years that have passed, it all happened rapidly; it's difficult to re-tell my story. I was walking through an alley in our village on an errand for my mother who had sent me to the open market to buy spices for our evening meal. Before I realized what was happening, I was lifted off my feet and roughly thrown onto a saddled horse. A coarsely woven, knotted scarf was quickly wrapped around my neck, leaving me no time to shout. The rider, a man who I could not see, held me with one hand by the tail of the scarf from behind and the reins of his horse with the other. If I tried to jump off and flee to save myself, I would clearly be dragged and trampled under the hooves of the horse, or strangled by the knotted cloth. Although I was terrified and found it difficult to breathe, I grabbed and held fast to the horse's mane, to save myself from this hideous fate. As we sped through the village gates, leaving behind the only home I had ever known, there was no time to think about anything other than staying on the horse. I quickly began to pray that my father and brothers would notice my absence and come looking for me.

Still the man held me tightly by the throat. It took every bit of my life force to hold myself upright and avoid crashing to my death. Leaving the village, we fled across the desert sands. The late morning heat had become unbearable and my captor did not offer any water to drink. Facing straight ahead I watched the sun begin a slow glowing descent over the horizon of the landscape. I still remember my relief when dusk began to fall, slowly cooling the intense heat of the day. Our horses fell in behind a caravan of merchants, riding and driving pack camels. Peering around I could see only a vast expanse of desert. Although the hold on my throat had loosened a bit, there was now no place for me to run.

As darkness overtook the caravan, I heard shouts from men bringing the camels to a halt. Rudely dumped from the horse onto the hot desert sand, lying on my back, I watched my captor dismount. This was my first glimpse of him. Grabbing me by the arm, he towed me to the place where men were setting up camp. My legs and feet had little feeling and I stumbled alongside, trying to keep up with him. Those who were making camp unloaded huge striped woolen bags containing carpets that were spread over the sand. The men made faces and crude gestures at me, laughing as I approached. My captor shouted obscenities at them and pushed me facedown onto a carpet where I instantly passed out from exhaustion.

Smells of roasting meat awakened me in the pitch dark of night. The cooking fire provided scant light. Afraid to move and ignoring my intense hunger, I huddled deeper into the carpet seeking any possible warmth in the cold, night air. Staring up into an endless, starry blanket of sky, I felt vulnerable in a way that I had never experienced in my short thirteen years of life. It was no mystery what was bound to befall me and I was very much afraid. One of the men passed by to relieve himself and saw that I was awake. He called out to my captor who promptly appeared, looming over me. He savagely grabbed my arm, hauling me up on to my feet. Pointing at the cooking fire, he insisted I eat and drink. Nothing had ever tasted so good to me as those first searing bites of meat, which burned the roof of my mouth. Someone tossed me a filthy burnoose and told me to put it on. As I ate, the men re-loaded the camels with their burdens. Once again I was thrown up on to a horse. My captor had my horse on the end of a rope that he again led from his own steed. Still, I had not been able to have a good look at him and I could see only his back. We traveled for many hours through the chilly darkness of night. Often, passing in and out of a sleep state and jolted awake in alarm, I had to rouse myself before falling off my horse.

At first light, the men began to call out. On the

edge of my vision in the distance I could barely make out the image of tall date palms, like pencil drawings scratched on the sky. As dawn progressed into morning the camels began to trot and we on horseback rushed across the sands into the shade of the caravansary and the promise of water. Much to my astonishment, a huge white tent was erected nearby. Rhythmic sounds of drums, bells, music, singing and enticing scents of cooked food were emanating from the huge domed tent.

My captor instructed me to remain on my horse as he approached the well in the center of the oasis. Before he could reach the water, a large man dressed in a richly appointed white robe emerged from the tent and in a loud voice ordered him to stop. They exchanged angry words and then all was calm. By this time, the entire caravan had entered the oasis, and we watched the camels making a mad rush to drink. When they were sated and unloaded, the huge beasts as well as most of the men lay down and quickly fell into a deep sleep.

I was taken into the tent and told to be silent. It was hard to hold my tongue as I beheld the opulent interior. Under my filthy bare feet, the entire floor was covered in soft, deeply woven, jewel-toned carpets in brilliant shades of ruby red and deep indigo blues. Richly hued cloth draperies such as I had never seen hung from the walls. Women adorned in gold and silver jewelry and bells which hung from their ankles, appeared carrying trays covered with foods which I could not identify. The scent of this food sent me into a swoon, and I collapsed onto the carpeted floor.

Awakened from my torpor, I found myself entirely unclothed. A woman was gently washing my body with cool, rose-scented water. Hastily attempting to cover my nakedness, I was soothed by the voice of the woman assuring me that I was now safe. She encouraged me to lie still telling me "You must quickly regain your former good health so you will be appealing to Sheik Zayed. You are very thin, we must fatten you up." Other lavishly dressed women came to me with indescribably succulent bits of food which one woman fed to me with her fingers, until finally I pushed her hand away and fell into a sound sleep. Once again, I awoke to the feeling of human hands on my body. This time the feeling was very pleasurable and I was not alarmed. One of the women was rubbing jasmine-scented oil onto every inch of me, including the soles of my feet. "You are such a lucky girl to have been purchased by the sheik." My abductor had sold me for an exorbitant price as a virgin bride. I was now the property of Sheik Zayed. My future husband had already amassed a harem of six wives. I was to become number seven.

The women carefully dressed my scrubbed and polished body in finery such as I had never imagined. They clothed me in an elegant dress richly embroidered with golden thread, my face hidden beneath a bejeweled niqab through which only my eyes could be seen. Gold and silver bracelets, which made a lovely tinkling sound when I moved, encircled both my wrists and ankles. Throughout the day my every need was fulfilled as servants of the sheik stood by to do my bidding. Upon hearing that dinner and the celebrations were about to start, I felt very nervous. My entire body broke out into glistening beads of fear-induced sweat that emanated the scent of jasmine flowers. A group of women appeared, taking me into the main chamber of the tent where Sheik Fayed awaited my arrival. As I entered the chamber, women began to shriek and create an eerie haunting sound with their mouths and fingers as music began to play. I was escorted to Sheik Fayed, who indicated that I should sit down next to him. He did not speak to me or make any move to touch me. Fayed was very handsome, but I could not tell if he had straight or curly hair as his head was covered with a patterned keffiyeh tied with traditional black cording. But his eyes were kind and he smiled as I sat, showing beautiful white teeth under a thick black mustache. When he clapped his hands the drumming and dancing began. Many women dressed in an immodest fashion were wearing only sparkling coverings over their breasts and delicate, sheer blousy pants adorned with glittering anklets hung with tiny bells. During their performance, I noticed several of the women holding aloft brass finger cymbals, striking them rhythmically in time to the sounds of drumming. As their beautiful bodies undulated like snakes to the sound of the drums, I found it difficult to sit still. Servants of the sheik plied me with delectable morsels of food and wine in a pretty silver cup, which was continually refilled until I began to feel very sleepy.

When at last I opened my eyes feeling an uncomfortable throbbing in my head, I was more than surprised to find myself comfortably ensconced within a silken howdah hung with fringes, secured on top of a camel. As we moved through the silent moonlit night of the desert, the rocking sway of the camel beneath reminded me of a baby in its mother's arms. A deep welling up of sadness and longing for my mother arose and I vowed to find her again one day. Comforted by the swaying of the camel I was lulled back into a sleep dream, traveling on my way into the unknown.

Serendipity

aurie was over the moon. Jared her gorgeous and charming boyfriend, had invited her to his work-related party. He must—she reasoned—be getting serious, to have asked her to accompany him to such a prestigious event. Jared promised to introduce her to all his co-workers and others involved with his industry. The party would be black tie, held in the grand ballroom of the most elegant hotel in town. His suggestion to take her shopping for an evening dress was too good to be true. She could barely believe her good luck.

When they had a mutual day off, the couple drove to the city for a romantic lunch. Pleasantly satiated with oysters, cold sauvignon blanc and warm sunshine on a deck overlooking the bay, they set off to find the perfect dress. In a mellow mood, Jared told Laurie *not* to look at price tags. "The sky's the limit today."

Taking their time, they meandered in and out of

small fashion boutiques and large department stores, looking for the exact right thing. Stepping out of the dressing room in an exclusive designer shop, she modeled a clingy pale blue sheath dress for Jared. The blue dress emphasized her large sapphire eyes, and they both knew they had found it. Laurie was thrilled when Jared told her how sexy she looked in the slim, blue dress. "My friends will be totally knocked out." Then he took her home, asking her to put on the dress again, only to see how quickly he could remove it.

On the morning of the long-anticipated event Laurie visited a luxurious beauty spa courtesy of Jared, got the works and emerged, feeling fabulous. That night Jared arrived right on time to pick her up. Raving about how gorgeous she looked, they went on to the hotel. In the car he related stories of boyhood escapades with his best friend Matt. She would, he felt sure, become friends with Matt's girlfriend, Nora.

The ballroom was every bit as elegant as Laurie had imagined. Tuxedoed waiters passed delectable hors d'oeuvres and tall crystal flutes of bubbling champagne. When Jared elbowed her and nodded in the direction of the door, they both gasped as Matt and Nora made their entrance. Spotting them, Laurie was horrified and tears filled her eyes. Nora was wearing a dress identical to her own, the ultimate social embarrassment. As the couple approached, the girls silently took a hard look at each other. Then Nora—throwing her arms around Laurie—began laughing merrily. Linking arms, they confidently strode toward the bar in their brightly colored spike heels, leaving the boyfriends standing speechless and wide-eyed in amazement.

Riley's Very Best Day Ever

When his person Jim appeared with the leash and called out "Hey Riley, let's go for a ride," Riley's entire body began to wag with happiness. Thrusting out his stocky black neck so that Jim could attach the leash he thought, *oh boy oh boy oh boy* and cheerfully loped alongside the person he loved best, out to the red Jeep parked in the driveway.

When Jim opened the door to the passenger side in the backseat, Riley leaped right in and off they went to the dog park. It was early. Riley had loved his breakfast of kibble sprinkled with bits of Jim's toast and his tummy felt really good.

There were no other dogs in the park when they arrived. But the smells!

When Jim closed the gate and unsnapped his leash, Riley made a mad dash for the nearest tree and marked his spot, just to prove that he had been there.

Jim settled in on a park bench painted in rainbow colors and took a bright pink Frisbee out of his backpack. Meanwhile Riley was making the rounds with his nose in everything. Suddenly, out of the corner of his eye he caught a glimpse of the Frisbee sailing toward him and took off running. When it hit the ground, he snapped it up and returned it to Jim, who immediately spun it high in the air. Riley sprinted after it. Leaping as high up as his four legs would fly him, he caught the pink disk in mid-air and raced back to Jim. After a few rounds of this game Riley was panting and the Frisbee was dripping wet.

Just about the time he lay down to catch his breath, the park gate opened to reveal a freckle-faced girl with bouncy orange curls leading a fancy white poodle on a rhinestone studded leash. When Riley trotted over to sniff her, the poodle shyly backed away, standing obediently by her girl. The girl took off the poodle's leash and still they stood quietly side-by-side just watching.

Then the parking lot began to fill up and the action hit the fan. Lots of dogs proceeded to drag their owners in behind them, jump up and down impatiently or lag along nervously as they viewed the wild scene in the park. A fluffy black and white Aussie Shepherd with one blue eye hot-footed it over to Riley snatching away the Frisbee, taking it straightaway to *his* person who threw it back across the park.

A pure joyful doggy feeling surrounded the entire pack of pooches as they ran to claim the pink prize! It was all in good fun as a sweet and fluffy golden retriever claimed the toy and dutifully returned it to *her* person. And so it went as a dignified Collie, gangly Great Dane and a wiggly Beagle, dropping the purple ball she had been carrying in her mouth each took a turn. Good-natured Riley was having such a doggone good time that he didn't even mind sharing his toy. Finally, when they all stopped to catch their breath, an adorable little black and tan dachshund proudly snapped up the pink Frisbee and toddled over to deliver the Frisbee back to Riley. What a day *oh boy oh boy oh boy* Riley was beat!

Back in the Jeep Jim tossed him his favorite green dog cookie and rolled down the window so Riley could hang his head out in the breeze on the way home. *hot dog that felt good* Smiling his biggest doggy smile, with his ears blown straight back in the wind Riley concluded that this had been his very best day ever.

Pickup

Entering a noisy bar, the tall blond woman looked around for the man in the photo. Not seeing him, she sat down at a table. They had met on a dating site. Never having done this kind of thing before, she thought, "People hook up on these sites every day, there's not really anything wrong with it." Remembering the various couples she knew, who when asked, "Where did you meet?" had told her sometimes sheepishly, that they met at a bar and later got married.

After messaging back and forth and exchanging snapshots, she and her correspondent had agreed to meet. Now here she was. Then she spotted him, coming through the front door. He looked exactly like his picture. "Well," she thought, "at least he was truthful about that." Nevertheless, her disappointment was instant; she knew the evening would be far from thrilling. She hoped that at least he would be a nice guy.

After introducing themselves, they chatted about their jobs and other small trivialities. She was comfortable enough, though not particularly interested in what he had to say. Her attention wandered. After the waiter took their order and the food was served, they began to eat. She nibbled her salad while he devoured his burger. It was a nice break from having to make small talk. Glancing up as she lifted the fork to her mouth, she noticed a man across the room staring at her. Ignoring him, it occurred to her that just trying to get through yet another first date was taking all of her energy.

When they were finished eating and her date suggested another glass of wine, she declined, telling him she had planned an early start the next morning. They paid their separate checks and rose to leave. When they got to the door, he went out and she stayed behind.

Heading back to the bar, she sat on a stool ordering another glass of wine, glad to have made it through the date. That was when the man who had been staring at her came to the bar and sat down next to her. They began to chat, and ended up howling with laughter. After a couple of drinks, he said to her in a husky voice, "Let's get outta here."

Unselfconsciously looking him straight in the eye she got right up and began to put on her coat.

Cheated

After the war ended in 1945, my mother and her sister Gerty served a blue-eyed Navy Seabee, hot coffee and donuts at the San Francisco USO. For years afterward, Auntie Gerty got a kick out of retelling the story about my dad following the pretty sisters home on the bus that night, and how the rest was history.

Their Jewish parents had immigrated from Eastern Europe, fleeing Russia at the turn of the century. Creating a new life in New York City, they had three boys and two girls. When the children were young, the family moved to Northern California from the East Coast, where nine first cousins from that close-knit family still live.

Of all the children in her family, my mother was the only one to marry outside of the Jewish faith. I'm unsure of my grandparents' reaction to her engagement, but I cherish the memories of loving acceptance my father always received from my mother's family and friends.

My father's large family grew up in a strict Southern Baptist tradition in the Oklahoma Territory before it became a state. He was one of nine siblings. Because of my father's infrequent visits to Oklahoma, I had limited opportunities to meet his extended family. As a result, I was raised in the loving embrace of a large Jewish family in the San Francisco Bay Area. Along with my parents, I attended every holiday dinner and festivity with my mother's family and was present at numerous weddings, funerals, bar mitzvahs and bat mitzvas.

When I was still in elementary school, we moved from San Francisco to Marin County, building a home in a developing suburban neighborhood. A small Baptist church was built on our corner shortly after we moved into our new home. Since I lacked any knowledge of my parents' discussions about religion, I only remember our small family soon joining that Baptist congregation. I sang in the choir and went to Sunday school and vacation bible school in the summers. My Mother and I were both baptized as Baptists inside that church and I wore a small gold cross on a delicate chain around my neck. My Mother never chose to share her thoughts or feelings about religion with me and I was given no information about the nature of her religious convictions, why she chose to convert to Christianity or any reaction she might have received from anyone in her family about her conversion. It seemed to me that she was much more concerned with what she wore to church and how I was dressed, than any convictions she may have held on the Christian teachings of the church.

Within a few short years, I began to question my affiliation with the Baptist church. With family, my Jewish identity felt real, but my mother's reluctance in teaching me Jewish history and traditions meant my understanding of Judaism came gradually over the years, in listening to aunts, uncles, and cousins. Although we attended Passover and Hanukkah dinners at the homes of my mother's brothers and sisters, I never truly understood the origins of the holidays and it didn't seem to make that much difference to me as a child. All the cousins were very close. My cousins have always felt more like brothers and sisters to me. My Jewish family always made me feel cherished and loved—a good thing for an only child.

Approaching my teen years, I questioned my mother about our relationship to the Jewish faith and its history, but I can't remember having any meaningful conversations about religion, and she never explained Jewish traditions to me. I felt that she always avoided and sidestepped the discussions that I longed for, and eventually I came to resent not having my questions taken seriously.

In high school we studied Buddhism in a Humanities class where I took a serious interest in theology and could share questions and discourse with my teacher and other students on religious topics. Although I was able to quote the bible chapter and verse and knew the lyrics to every Christian hymn, eventually my hot, rebellious teenaged brain completely rejected any further possibility of a relationship with Christianity. I denounced my conversion as coercion by my parents and often found myself angry. My consciousness retained an interest in Buddhist studies, and I have often described myself as a JewBu. Throughout my life I've studied and explored many different faiths and religions and have been known to say, "I take a very wide view on theology," but when asked in specific about my religion I always state, "I am Jewish."

For many years I've wrestled with the question of why my mother converted to Christianity, had me baptized and refused to discuss her feelings about Judaism with me. Is it possible that the horrifying consequences of the holocaust during World War II instilled such a deep fear of her Jewishness that she abandoned her religious heritage or refused to share it with her daughter? While this is something I'll never know, the lifelong impact on me, a daughter of Judaism deprived of her birthright has created a lifetime of confusion, guilt and resentment.

Acute Heartburn

Standing on a corner waiting for the crossing signal to change, a blue car passed, triggering a nasty burning sensation shooting up the back of my throat. The first time I saw his car I was parked in the church parking lot on a Sunday morning. I'll *never* forget the feeling I had as he opened the door to that blue car and stepped out. You hear about love at first sight, but I couldn't imagine it ever happening to me. I actually felt my heart expanding, throbbing, opening in a brand-new sensation that left me giddy and short of breath. Later, I discovered his name was James—a name I would hold close to my dizzy heart.

At the end of the church service, many of us trickled into the community room for coffee and there he was. Lanky and sandy-haired, dressed in jeans, a plaid flannel shirt and a fleece vest. I pretended not to notice him, but he wasted no time approaching, offering a hot cup of coffee along with a disarming smile. His piercing blue eyes quickly took me in from head to toe, eliciting an uncontrollable blush. Trying to regain composure, I took the paper cup. "Thanks, I could kill for some hot coffee right now."

"Luckily you won't need to do anything so drastic. Hi pretty girl, my name's James."

At the time I was in a comfortable relationship with a guy named Jared who was good looking, polite and reliable. Jared took me to nice places and would bring me flowers—a really nice guy. But once James asked me out, I didn't think twice about throwing Jared under the bus. So stupid.

It did not begin innocently, because we were instantly in lust. That's how I became so familiar with that blue car. I would spend a lot of time getting all dressed up for a date, but later I'd emerge from his car in a disheveled state and stagger back up the steps to my apartment in a void of bliss, uncaring of my appearance.

When we went out James was attentive and even sometimes publicly affectionate, so people began to understand that we were a couple. My girlfriends would say things like, "Wow, you are absolutely radiant!" and I felt radiant. In the recesses of my mind I heard wedding bells, but kept those thoughts strictly to myself. I didn't want to jinx it. Instead, I threw myself into decorating mode for the onset of finding our perfect abode. James, however, found a fault in all the properties we inspected. Nevertheless, I continued to purchase and pour over copies of Architectural

Digest. I was really into it. Maybe I had found a new calling as a real estate stager?

All relationships eventually begin to cool off following the initial hot flash of intimacy. When I noticed the first signs of this I just went out and bought a bunch of sexy lingerie, thinking it would be easy to reignite that old excitement.

One evening on my way home from work under a clear sky studded with twinkling stars, I spotted him on the street illuminated under a lamppost, locked in a passionate embrace with a woman I couldn't identify. A flood of tears blinded me as I drove home. To say that I was devastated would be a massive understatement. Lying on the bed in which James and I had torn up countless times in mad bouts of lovemaking, I sobbed uncontrollably, confused and miserable.

It was then that the sudden attacks of heartburn arose unbidden at odd hours. Later, when I confronted James he was casual and unapologetic telling me, "I realize now that being in a monogamous relationship will just never work for me. I do love you. Why don't we try an open relationship?"

The following week when I went downstairs to check my mail, I discovered a fancy, engraved invitation to Jared's wedding.

Mine All Mine

They met on the Euro rail between Germany and Belgium in 1969. Ingrid, a pretty Swedish girl with silky blond hair and bright blue eyes, bumped into Lucca while boarding the train. Struggling up the stairs loaded down with luggage, she found herself crushed against a young man crowned with an explosion of jet-black curls. Quickly apologizing, she looked up into his dark liquid chocolate eyes and was smitten at once. Without thinking he reached down to help with the baggage and steady her onto her feet.

Moving into the passenger car, the curly-haired stranger inquired if he might help lift her carry-on suitcase to an overhead compartment. She smiled, sliding into the window seat as he sat down beside her. Their marriage was marked by the frequent retelling of this story.

Lucca was a student at the University of Milan, majoring in classical music and voice. He was on his way home, using his rail pass to visit various sights of interest throughout Europe during his school break. Seated in the cozy, swiftly moving train they chatted, sharing travel stories. He was curious about the vibrant, golden-haired girl on holiday from Sweden, asking her to tell him stories about her homeland in Scandinavia. Communicating in words pieced together from their native Italian, Swedish and bits of other languages along with the movement of their hands, they found themselves to be quite companionable, eventually making their way to the dining car, sharing wine, a sandwich and more conversation.

As the train approached the Belgium/France border, the two young people agreed to exchange mailing addresses. When they came to the crossroads of their parting and agreed to keep in touch, Lucca wrapped his arms around Ingrid and whispered in her ear, "Nos volveremos a encontrar" (We will meet again), kissed her pale cheek and disembarked for Italy. Ingrid always recalled, "…feeling my heart flip over as I watched Lucca leave the train."

Following the completion of her degree at the University of Stockholm, Ingrid was bound for Paris to begin a job as an au pair, for a Parisian family with three children. In response to his inquiry about her new job, she wrote back, "I adore working with children." "This is my dream-come-true."

Arriving at the Gare de Lyon, her new Parisian family stood gathered at the station to meet her.

Madame and Monsieur LeGrande and their three adorable children Claude, Louis and Claire seemed equally as excited to be hosting a beautiful Swedish Au Pair, as Ingrid was to be there. Viewing the sights of the fabled City of Light through the windows of their Citroen, Ingrid could barely sit still. The children chattered nonstop, while Madame and Monsieur appeared satisfied with their new au pair. Everything was perfect as they arrived at the LeGrande home.

Throughout the first year of her arrival in Paris, letters continued to arrive from Lucca in Milan. They visited during holidays and Ingrid soon realized that she had her first serious boyfriend. After Lucca graduated and proposed marriage, Ingrid called her parents to announce the news. "Oh Mor, Lucca has asked me to marry him and I've accepted. Papa, I'm so excited, and we've agreed to have many children." The future Swedish grandparents were thrilled.

Their large, festive wedding was attended by all of Lucca's Italian friends, neighbors and family members, as well as many members of Ingrid's extensive Scandinavian family and of course the Le Grande family, all pleased to have an Italian holiday in the sun.

Near the university, where Lucca now worked as a cellist for the famous Milan Symphony Orchestra, they found their first apartment. The young newlyweds blended seamlessly into Milanese city life. With lots of help and support from Lucca's family and lifelong friends in Milan, they developed a rich social life in the charming Italian city. But try as they may, no babies presented themselves on their horizon. Ingrid, it was discovered, was unable to have children. Not allowing this fact to deter their happiness as a couple, Ingrid and Lucca explored Europe whenever they found free time. Often, the topic of adoption arose in their conversations. They investigated the possibility of visiting orphanages and adoption agencies in the various countries in which they planned to travel.

By the time the couple had entered into their mid-thirties, the result of their worldwide travels had morphed into a large and diverse family. Mama Ingrid and Papa Lucca discovered their first daughter Janie at an orphanage in India. The sight of babies crying in rows of cribs made it clear they were making a positive choice. When Ingrid reached for little Janie and saw those tiny arms reach out, she was a goner. As the years passed, their family substantially increased with the adoptions of adorable children from Japan, Greece, Russia, Ireland and Vietnam along with Janie from India. Their unique family was the talk of Milan, where they had by now built a sprawling home to accommodate all of the kids. Ingrid and Lucca were lauded as models of parenthood.

Everywhere they went people repeatedly asked them, "Which one is yours?" To which, In a firm and convincing voice Ingrid would always reply with a big smile, **"They are mine — all mine!"**

Superstition

Poor Jenny. Every time I was invited over to her house to play, Jenny's mom bugged the heck out of her all day long. I still feel sorry for her. It seemed like whatever we did, Jenny's mom would guilt-trip her and scare us into being nice little children.

The family came from somewhere in the south. Their accents and habits seemed different from that of my own California born and bred clan. Her mother was especially careful about what she said and did. If she was in the kitchen cooking and happened to spill a bit of salt, she would immediately pick up a pinch, toss it back over her shoulder and then knock on some wood. These actions, she told me, were to ward off bad luck. My own mother would have "pitched a fit"—a term I picked up at Jenny's house—at having to clean up the mess.

This concept of "bad luck" was the very thing that seemed to consume my friend Jenny.

As a seven-year-old, I had many reasons to cherish

Jenny as my best friend. To say that she was a very good girl was a vast understatement. I could always be sure that she would never, ever tell a lie or, as she told me "I'll go straight to hell." I could trust her completely. When other kids would straight-out fib with their fingers crossed behind their backs, I could be sure that Jenny would never stoop to that level. Yet, when hoping for the best on any outcome she would leave me saying "Don't worry, I'll have my fingers and toes crossed for you today."

One day we were walking down the street when a pitch-black cat scooted across the sidewalk in front of us. In a flash Jenny started to cry, which caught me completely off guard. I thought that maybe she had been stung by a bee or stepped in some dog poo. "Now my day is completely ruined," she lamented, tears streaming down her rosy little cheeks. Still, I didn't get it. "Having a black cat cross your path is just the worst. Now some kind of terrible bad luck will surely happen to me today. My mom will just freak out when I tell her!" Then she began to caution me about avoiding the cracks in the sidewalk, "It could break your mother's back." When I mentioned that it was Friday the 13th, she flipped out. "This is the most dangerous day ever on the calendar. Something awful can happen on Friday the 13th. Be *really careful* about everything that you do for the rest of the day."

Upstairs in Jenny's bedroom, snuggled up under warm quilts when I was sleeping over, we were reading *Grimm's Fairy Tales* to each other and discussing the morals of the stories. Jenny placed a high value on morality. She could always give me examples of right and wrong. But when I asked for the reasoning or proof behind these ideals she would always say, "Just because…" Usually the witches or bad people would die and the children would get a treat, or the frog who kissed the princess would turn into a handsome prince. The stories were all about blindly believing in good and evil.

We were playing dolls on her back lawn when Jenny glanced up. "Red sky in morning, sailor take warning." Look at the sky it's fixin' to rain." We had no sooner made umbrella forts for the dolls when sure enough, rain began to fall and we ran for Jenny's kitchen door. When I stepped in with my umbrella still open, Jenny's mom, who was standing at the sink peeling potatoes, started to scream. Close that umbrella girl! Don't you know any better than to bring an open umbrella into the house? This could bring a curse down on our family. Who knew? My own mother would have only nagged me to wipe my feet before coming in.

We went upstairs and snuck into her mom's stash of make-up. First, she made up my face and then I did hers. When I held up the hand mirror from her parent's dresser, Jenny turned to see and bumped into me. I dropped the mirror on the hardwood floor and it cracked. Jenny totally freaked out and yelled at me.

Her mom came running up the stairs to see what was wrong. When she saw us all made up "Like wanton women," and then saw the broken mirror on the floor—well that was it!

Roughly scrubbing my face with soap, she told me to "Skedaddle and don't ever come back. Thanks to you, now we're cursed with 100 years of bad luck and will need to move to another house to get rid of it." That was the end of my relationship with Jenny who was forbidden to ever play with me again and now even snubbed me for the remainder of the school year. Naturally I was heartbroken. It was a tough transition between third and fourth grades and a lonely summer vacation.

I did a lot of thinking during that long and hot summer. What did I learn from all of this? Well—you just can't be too careful.

Evie's Shadows

Long shadows spread across the plank floor on the old, weather-beaten front porch. The moon, making its nightly appearance, illuminated the garden with a gentle glow. Her favorite floral chintz cushion in the white wicker rocker felt just right. With the tip of her toe, she rocked herself, causing Evie's long chestnut hair to sway back and forth in the evening breeze.

Memories were a lot like shadows. You just never knew where they would appear, or for how long. Gazing out at her rose garden in the dusky waning light, she allowed her mind to wander back in time. She had grown up in this house and memories presented themselves everywhere she looked. This time she was having a *good* memory — envisioning her mom, in her sun hat and gardening gloves, pruning the roses. Mom loved those roses, and each summer they would reward her with a riot of color and scent. Like a jewelry box of colored gemstones, the roses budded out in otherworldly shades of red, orange, yellow, purple and everything in between. People passing by would stop and hang their heads over the little picket fence just to breathe in the heavenly scent emanating from their flowers. The lovely fragrance of roses enveloped her tonight.

Evie missed her mom, but not her father or his brother, her Uncle Seth. Those painful memories, despite her attempts to forget them, surfaced, casting long dark shadows over her heart and making her sad and very angry. One day when Evie was maybe four years old—she would never, ever forget—her mom had gone out to do the grocery shopping. Dad was watching TV in his old leather recliner and she was playing with toys on the floor near his feet. Reaching down he picked her up, sat little Evie on his lap and began jiggling her around. Evie giggled, but before she knew what was happening, he had unzipped his pants and was rubbing her bottom against something hard on his lap. His ragged breath came faster and faster. Letting out a long moan, he roughly dropped the little girl on the floor. That was the beginning of the time when she never wanted to be alone with him, ever again. "Don't tell your mom or we'll both be in big trouble." Little Evie tried to stay away from him, but he always caught her. As she got older, it made her feel sick when Dad called her his "special girlfriend." Each time *it* happened, her loathing for him increased. She hated herself too, but to spare her mother, Evie kept the secret. She grew into a very quiet and withdrawn child who had a difficult time making friends.

When she was about ten, Dad's brother Seth came to live with them. Uncle Seth needed a place to live close to his job at the auto parts store. Seth was a big, rough guy who worked out at the gym. When he was at home, he usually had a can of beer in his hand. Soon, the ugliness started with Uncle Seth. Her uncle was often drunk, stinking of beer and cigarettes. Evie hated all of it, and she avoided being near him.. Her attempts to resist only resulted in him punching her where the bruises wouldn't show, so she stopped even trying and just lay very still until he was through with her.

Her mother came home early one afternoon and caught Uncle Seth lying on top of her. Mom had a fit and kicked him out of the house on the spot. Evie hoped things would improve, but she was mistaken. When she tried to explain what Dad had been doing, Mom cried and told Evie that she "…better not tell any more lies!" After that, mom cracked down on her, demanding that her daughter wear very plain clothing and never allowing her to wear any make-up, not even lipstick. When Evie returned home one morning after a slumber party, Mom noticed the shiny pink polish on her fingers and toes. "Go upstairs and take that right off before your father gets home and sees it!" That was the last time she was allowed to stay out overnight.

When she started high school, mom and dad made it very clear that dating would be out of the question. "We better not *ever* catch any boys hanging around here!"

A school counselor, alerted by teachers that Evie was a loner, advised her to join some clubs in school. She signed up to work on the school newspaper and discovered that being a reporter was fun. She could roam around the campus in her free time and wrote articles for the school paper. Her journalism teacher told her she had writing talent. Each time she saw her byline in the school paper, it cheered her up. Her schoolmates took notice, and little by little she made some friends. They called her "the quiet girl" at school.

A tall blond boy named Jim on the newspaper staff occasionally sat with her at lunchtime in the cafeteria. They enjoyed spending time in journalism class putting the paper together. It seemed only natural when Jim suggested going for a milkshake after school. Evie and Jim started spending a lot more time together. Her girlfriend Sally told Evie that the kids at school assumed they were "an item." Evie, of course, could not imagine herself having a boyfriend. Besides—her parents would kill her.

As time went on, it became harder and harder for Evie to deny her feelings for Jim. They sneaked off to be alone whenever they could. Kissing was one thing, but when Jim wanted to touch her, Evie became very upset. She couldn't tell Jim about the awful things that had been going on in her family, sure that if he found out, he would stop loving her. She claimed to be a virgin with a belief in saving herself for marriage. Evie's parents seemed very relieved when they eloped soon after graduation. Jim and Evie were in love, and Evie felt a sense of safety and contentment she had never known.

Jim enjoyed going out with his buddies after work for a drink, and Evie soon discovered that her husband was a mean drunk. He would come home and fire questions at her. "What have you been doing all day? Who did you see?" He was jealous beyond belief and didn't even want her to visit her parents. Then Jim accused her of being attracted to other guys and demanded that she stay in the apartment when he was at work. His jealous fury escalated beyond mere verbal abuse. When he began to beat her up and then rape her, she truly considered taking her own life. Jim was worse than Uncle Seth and her father combined.

Evie hoped and prayed for a baby. *He'll love me and stop hurting me if I can give him a child.* Holding on to this thought was the only thing that made the violent rapes tolerable. But sadly, her hopes of becoming pregnant never came true and the terrible abuse continued.

Late one night, there was a knock at her front door. A city policeman drove Evie to the hospital after informing her of her husband's injuries from a bar fight. Someone had beaten Jim, and he was in a coma. He died from the head injuries two days later. Not long after Jim's death, Evie's father had a heart attack and passed away. Mom was inconsolable and asked Evie to come home and live with her.

Evie had never gotten past the pain of her mother's distrust after her childhood confession, but it was time to let bygones be bygones and allow a chance for healing. Signing up for classes at the community college inspired her. She excelled and finished with a Library Sciences certificate, which led to a job at the local library. The pleasant balance between her peaceful life at home and her work at the library made life much more tolerable.

Mom had not been feeling very well. The doctor's diagnosis revealed lung cancer caused by secondhand smoke from her husband's lifetime smoking habit. Evie became her mother's caregiver, driving her to medical appointments and being responsible for her many medications. Before long, the illness became very advanced, and her mother needed constant care. The library offered her flexible hours. Her mother's death left Evie with the house and garden.

She was grateful this evening to be wrapped in the comfortable embrace of her familiar childhood home. Dark memories came and went, but no one could hurt her ever again. This was enough for her.

Man's Best Friend

Footprints leading down to the swiftly flowing river were visible even through the dense, misty fog. There was no doubt about it, he had come this way. How he got the boat out during that raging summer storm last night was a mystery to me.

Yesterday had started just like any other day on our lazy stretch of the riverbank. Sunlight trickling in through the curtains beckoned us awake. The only thing missing was the sound of Jasper whining at the door, asking to come in. Padding to the entryway in my house slippers, I opened the door and there was our dog Jasper, lying dead in a pool of blood on the front walk. My husband Tom jumped out of bed and came running at the sound of my scream. Standing there in his pajamas and bare feet, he let out an ugly howl, his eyes darting around wildly in a panic looking for the shooter.

Oh my god—poor Jasper. Who would do this? "I don't know but I'm sure as hell gonna find out" Tom yelled, throwing on his clothes and storming out the door, shotgun in hand. I went back inside to change my clothes and get a blanket for my beloved buddy, but not before calling the sheriff to make a report. I proceeded to wrap Jasper in the blanket and carry him into the garage so other animals could not molest him. The next step was removing the pool of blood from my doorway. Hosing down the walkway took less time than I had expected, as the blood was still so fresh. Then I went to the kitchen to make coffee and waited for the authorities to arrive.

The sheriff came and went, looking at the photos and asking lots of questions that I could not answer. As the day progressed with no sign or word from Tom, my anxiety increased. Night fell and I was still alone with no husband and no dog. A serious fear took hold of me when another vicious summer storm whipped up, shaking and drenching my world. Lightning strikes cast eerie shadows onto the river with a brilliant glow.

The next morning, a loud knocking at my front door awakened me early after a restless night. Stumbling downstairs with sleep in my eyes, I found a couple of sheriffs demanding to know the whereabouts of my husband. Joseph Price, our neighbor, had been murdered in his barn. His bereaved wife Margie reported that our dog Jasper had been spotted the day before, trotting down the road with one of their chickens in his mouth. After that, no one seems to be sure exactly what happened. Later in the kitchen, a buzzing vibration from my cell phone alerted me to a text from Tom, "I'm OK." Nothing else. Now I was frantic.

Years rolled by with the people in our town always pointing fingers at me. I kept my head down and stayed close to home, spending a lot of time sitting on the riverbank — waiting. I never remarried or got another dog. No one ever saw or heard from Tom again.

Saga Of The Wild Burros

My friend Ishi owned a mule. Bonita was not just any mule. An exceptionally sleek and beautiful mule, she was trained for the show ring. Well-mannered, smart and very comfortable to ride, she would do just about anything asked of her—only better than any horse I ever met. Spoiled by the ultra-smooth gait of my Peruvian Paso horses over the years, I avoided riding most other breeds of horses, but it was always a pleasure to ride on Bonita.

The four of us were a team, patrolling the parks and trails—Ishi on Bonita and me on Mi Amigo. An unusual pair, our equine companions drew comments wherever we went. Amigo was pitch black, with a long, wavy mane drifting down to his shoulder. Little girls, dragging a parent in tow would come running up shouting, "Look Dad, it's the black stallion!" Always, we stopped to allow children to pet and talk to the horse and mule. But at other times, Amigo would not even get a second glance. Hikers on the trail would come right up to Bonita and ask us, "What kind of an animal is this?", prompting Ishi to launch into her favorite recitation on the virtues of mules. For years we rode, patrolled the trails and camped out with Bonita and Amigo. Bonita 'had a thing' for Amigo. When we would walk him out of the trailer, she would usually begin to squeal. We referred to the pair as Mr. and Mrs. Morse and I developed a special fondness for mules and donkeys.

Every summer, the Bureau of Land Management transports a load of mustangs and wild donkeys, also known as burros, to the fairgrounds in Santa Rosa and adopts them out for a modest fee. We would make it a point to attend these events, just to look at the livestock and see who went home with a new equine buddy. Mustangs are remarkably bright, hardy, and willing, and a special bond usually forms between the horse and its new owner. People often took the donkeys as pets, companions and protectors for their horses, or just for pasture ornaments. It was always quite a scene, witnessing the frightened, distrustful wild animals racing around, sending up clouds of dust in the makeshift fairground corrals. Watching, we would make predictions on which ones would be chosen.

On one of these occasions, I struck up a conversation with a horse wrangler, having developed a yen to own a burro. We received an invitation from the wrangler to tour the BLM ranch near Susanville, home to herds of wild horses and burros available for adoption. He gave me the paperwork for potential ownership and driving directions.

That day at the fairgrounds marked the beginning of our mission. Both of us would need to schedule time to overnight in Susanville, as the drive would take all day. On the morning that Ishi arrived at my place, we hitched the horse trailer to the back of my pickup, embarking bright and early with a stash of snacks, water and lots of good music. The route from Sonoma County was very straight-forward, taking us through Winters, Williams and Willows and on to Red Bluff and Redding, where the scenery really kicked in. We passed through Whiskeytown and Shasta Trinity National Recreation Area, where the panoramic landscape leading to Shasta Lake made the entire trip worthwhile. We oohed and aahed our way through the bucolic, awe-inspiring forest, enjoying views of the lakes and rivers along the way, finally bringing us to the main street of Susanville.

After checking into a modest motel on the main drag, we followed directions to the BLM to get our bearings before it got dark. Arriving at the BLM office, I presented my paperwork. After they deemed my home horse facility and trailer acceptable, we made an appointment to return the next morning to collect our adoptees.

Reveling in the freedom of our adventure, away from the responsibilities of everyday life, we went out for dinner and tossed back a few drinks, excited about our prospects for the next day. Fortunately, it would be impossible to get lost here on the main street, which was only one block long and we were able to make it back to the motel without incident.

In the morning, we enjoyed a big country breakfast and headed back to the BLM, located on the outskirts of town. They were expecting us. The hunky cowboy wranglers took us out to a huge corral, which enclosed dozens of mustangs and burros. "Take yer pick", they offered. We agreed that having a pair of companion burros would be better than taking just one. After wandering around for a while, checking out the livestock, I spotted an adorable foal that looked to be a few months old, standing next to her mother. I called out to the wranglers, "I want that little Jenny." Ishi chose an adult female saying, "Give me that one with the lightning stripes on her ears."

It was quite a sight, watching the cowboys wrangling those untamed, wild critters into my horse trailer. They backed my rig up to a ramp, where one guy stood at the end on the ground, with another straddled above. Somehow, other cowboys had singled out the little girls we had chosen, guiding them toward the ramp. As the burros came through, the guy on top reached down and slipped short ropes with identifying BLM numbers around their necks.

After they were prodded along into the trailer, the door was quickly slammed shut behind them. Those cowboys made it look easy, but believe me, you would not want to get kicked by one of those razor-sharp little hooves. I named them Jewel and Gem, as I am a jeweler by trade. The youngster was Little Jewel and the adult would be Gem.

It must have been easily ninety degrees departing Susanville that morning. We were astounded to be transporting two completely wild animals, which we could not touch. As the hours sped by with the heat rapidly rising, I began to wonder if I had made a big mistake? We would not be able to open the doors to provide our little captives with water. It must have been awfully hot in that trailer and I could never forgive myself if those innocent burros died on my watch. Occasionally we pulled over and climbing up on the wheel wells, peered in the overhead windows to make sure they were still standing.

When we returned home with our exotic cargo it was still light, but just barely. Anticipating this moment, we had in advance constructed a pipe corral paddock in a grass pasture, sliding an elongated steel water tank halfway under the fencing, to accommodate both the horses and donks on either side. Backing the rig flush up against the enclosure, one of us swung the corral gate in, while the other opened the back door of the trailer and sprinted away. When the door opened, those fuzzy little burros shot out into their new pasture and had a long cool drink.

Each day I would bring a folding chair and a book into the burro corral and sit for an hour, hoping that they would get used to me. I didn't ask them for anything. As the weeks passed, they still did not appear to trust me, moving away quickly as I quietly entered their space. I was no closer to bonding with them than the day they arrived. Yet, I noticed the rope on Little Jewel's neck tightening more and more. Because she was so small, it dragged on the ground. Occasionally she stepped on it and would gag herself. The situation was looking dangerous. I began to fear that she might strangle.

Panic set in and I called every large animal vet in the count asking if anyone would come with a sedation gun, so that we could get that rope off her neck. They all said no. Finally, a local, trusted vet said that if I could find someone to come with a gun to do the deed, he would provide a sedation pellet. The previous summer I had been a volunteer at Safari West Wildlife Preserve. It was a stretch, but I called a friend there and (the late) John Roberts, their wild animal handler, called me back. John was a great guy. I put him in touch with the vet and early the next morning they both showed up. Remembering everything as if in slow motion, I watched John go down on one knee in the grass, taking careful aim at Little Jewel. He shot the stun gun and we watched as she froze. Her long silky ears flopped over, and ever so slowly she sank to the ground. Confidently, John went to my baby burro and safely got rid of the dreadful rope. Then he got a hug from me. After that, Jewel began to gentle, so that I could slowly approach her with a carrot, she eventually becoming an affectionate pet. But Gem remained wild and aloof.

I drove up to feed the livestock early one morning and got the shock of my life. In the burro corral there were now three instead of two. Tossing out hay to the animals and as quickly as I could, gunned the truck back down to the house where I roused my husband out of bed. "You've got to come with me now—come on!" He was not amused. "Get your ass out of the bed and into the truck." He came along reluctantly, not one to appreciate being given an order. But when we got to the corrals, he burst out laughing and said he couldn't believe his eyes. Gem had fooled us and given birth to a baby Jack during the night. None of us, even the vet, had any clue that she was pregnant.

Calling Ishi to tell her the news, she replied in her typically dry, hilarious manner. "Good job Nance, ya got a twofer!"

Timing Is Everything

Despite her doctor inducing labor four hours earlier, Holly was still in labor. Her husband Tom sat at her bedside holding her hand, looking worried, with her tired and concerned mom sitting on the other side. The hospital staff hovered around, ensuring everything was in order. At this point she would have given anything for it to be over. Sleep, she just wanted to go to sleep. Then she heard her doctor say, "OK Holly, the head is crowning, get ready to push." With what seemed to her to be the very last bit of energy she would ever have, she bore down screaming and out came her baby girl.

The anticipated arrival was scheduled for February 28. But because of the extended length of the labor, the date was now February 29, a leap year. The nursing staff arranging flowers and admiring baby Annie as she nursed for the first time, told Holly how unusual it was to have a leap-year baby on their maternity floor. Too exhausted to give it much thought, she drifted off to sleep with her new daughter at her side.

Each year on Annie's birthday, everyone would make a big deal out of her leap-year birth date. A leap year has 366 days. The calendar gains an additional day every four years. A person born on a leap year, she was told, was theoretically only one-quarter of their actual age. So when her fourth birthday arrived, Annie was dismayed to hear that although she considered herself to be a big girl, she was actually only a one-year-old baby. This made her mad.

Annie would not let up. Why, she asked Holly over and over, wasn't she born on the 28th instead of the 29th? She didn't *want* to be a leap-year baby. The other kids teased her. Her birthday parties were always celebrated on February 28— not her real birthday. Even if they celebrated on March 1 she would still be a Pisces born in a leap year.

As the years went by, timing became more and more important for Annie. She obsessively calculated the timing of her every move and decision. If something went wrong, she blamed it on bad timing. Her credo was: "Timing is everything."

Annie had grown into a willowy, attractive young woman with wavy auburn hair and green eyes. People often commented on her good looks. They also noticed that she was secretive and elusive. One year on her birthday, a friend gifted her with a visit to an astrologer. When making her appointment with Louise the astrologer, she insisted that her appointment be scheduled on an astrologically auspicious day.

Louise had charted Annie's vital information and began their meeting saying, " I notice you are very intent on having all of your ducks in a row all the time." When Annie told her about being a leap-year baby and describing her "timing" theory, Louise replied, "In constantly forcing the issue of timing, you are fighting with yourself and fighting against the natural Pisces tendency to go with the flow. This could contribute to the making of mistakes. Do you feel as though you find yourself in uncomfortable situations without knowing how you got there?" Annie was stunned. This was the very issue in her life that consistently confounded her. By the time they had concluded their meeting, Annie was convinced that she needed to make some very real changes in her belief system.

Instead of listening to her gut feelings as she had vowed to do, she listened instead to her inner need to control. Her parents had an important anniversary coming up and she wanted to surprise them with a big party. Doing this without consulting her mom and dad was a huge mistake. After making all the arrangements and sending out invitations, she learned that close friends of her parents had already created and scheduled an anniversary party with them. Embarrassed and angry, she failed to attend what would be their last party together. Not long after, her dad passed away and Annie was devastated.

In the workplace she was an icon of order. All her co-workers knew she felt incapable of making a mistake and feared her. Flexibility was not part of her program. In her eyes, everything was either black or white with no gray areas.

One morning, checking the traffic patterns on her smart phone, she noticed that her regular route to work appeared to be clogged with slow traffic. Planning to outsmart the traffic, Annie set the GPS in her car and took off thinking that she would save some time by using an alternate route. The GPSs then proceeded to outsmart *her*, taking her far out of her way and causing her to be very late to work, missing a crucial business meeting. This provided her boss, who was sick of her control issues, a good reason to fire her on the spot.

Feeling her inner clock ticking, she spent a lot of time thinking about getting married and starting her own family. Setting her sights on a good-looking guy named Jack at her new job, she convinced a co-worker to create a time where she could meet Jack in a coincidental situation. When he showed up with a date, Annie was livid and never spoke to her co-worker friend again. After this story spread around the office, she was no longer invited to social gatherings.

Annie bumped into a tall, dark-haired guy while playing soccer in the park one warm spring Saturday morning, and they tumbled onto the grass. Although she was mortified, the guy lay on his back laughing uproariously. When she started to make a run for it, he reached over and grabbed her hand. Introducing himself, he said that his name was Pete. They sat on the grass in the sun chatting until Annie's teammates called her back to the game. Later, she was more than surprised to find that Pete had hung around after the game waiting for her. He asked her to join him for coffee and the rest is history.

Their completely unplanned meeting became the catalyst for a dramatic life change for Annie. After that she began to soften, remembering the words that Louise the astrologer had said to her so long ago. Annie and Pete married and had a little girl named Emily. Now she had everything she had ever wanted.

Watching her daughter playing with a schoolmate, Annie overheard Emily giving bossy orders to her little friend in a very controlling manner. When she stepped into the room with the girls, Emily asked her mom about the importance of making plans. "This is important, right mom?" Suddenly seeing in her daughter the part of herself she liked least, she took a deep breath, gave Emily her best advice and hoped that she would hear it. "Honey, follow your heart and happiness will follow."

Nancy & Nancy

One day a new client named Nancy arrived at my fitness studio, requesting a workout plan. She had noticed my horses grazing in their pasture on her way up the driveway and was curious to know what breed they were? As I got to know her, she told me about the horse farm at Sonoma Developmental Center, where she boarded her horse Fudge. SDC was only minutes from my place in Glen Ellen and was adjacent to Sonoma Valley Regional Park, with great trails for riding. Later I would join the Regional Parks Mounted Assistance Unit, the State Parks MAU and the SDC Mounted Posse. Logging in monthly patrol hours was a basic requirement for all three organizations, where I made many new friends.

For many years to come I would load a horse into my trailer and drive to one of the parks to ride whenever I had some free time. At first, I took Penguina, the adorable little black and white paint Peruvian mare, borrowed from my friend (the late)

Judy Collins, after losing my Peruvian Paso mare Asia. Often, I would meet up with Nancy to spend peaceful hours on the trail. She was a schoolteacher, who had married my old friend Richard, the piano-player and they had two young sons. Both hailed from the east coast. Nancy was very adventurous, always game for absolutely anything. She would go horse camping at the drop of a hat, tossing a can of tuna, a jar of peanut butter, a candy bar and a bottle of tequila into a sack and take off. Conversely, I would spend time the night before making up a batch of kosher tuna and hard-boiled egg with cucumber, the way my mother had made it adding capers for good measure, home-baked bread, chocolate truffles and a bottle of good wine to share. But in other ways we had a lot in common and would discuss movies, books, the state of the world and of course, horses.

Amigo's owners had mailed me a video from out-of-state, offering their gorgeous black, five-year-old gelding for sale. It showed him dancing around in an arena and included some photos of his mother, a tall, pitch black, registered Peruvian Paso mare. We shared dinner at my house and watched the video. Both of us were entranced with the feisty young gelding. Nancy was adamant. "You've got to have him!"

The two of us had been camping at the Stewart Ranch Horse Camp on the edge of Point Reyes National Seashore. Out there on the vast, lush lands of the national seashore, one could ride for days and never cross the same trail twice. The west Marin scenery is awe-inspiring and majestic, encompassing a variety of densely wooded, indescribably scenic terrain from mountaintops to the sea. In my saddlebags I always carried binoculars—handy for gazing up into the tops of gigantic redwoods to view an eagle's nest, or spy on the agile snow-white deer and wild elk that populated this area. Other mandatory equipment included: a head lamp, should we find ourselves still riding when night fell— treacherous!, a first aid kit in case of the inevitable injury, a package of Benadryl in the event we unwittingly blundered into the ubiquitous stinging nettles that abounded in the Pt. Reyes forests, a multi-use knife, water and snacks.

On a warm and crystal-clear morning, we awoke in our tent and decided to make the all-day trip down to Wildcat Beach and back. It was hot and there was a pond where we could cool off and have our lunch on the way down. Maybe halfway down the trail, passing only a few other riders, we were astonished to see a saddled, riderless horse galloping furiously up the trail. Courageous young women, we jumped down from our own horses, arms akimbo in an attempt to block the trail and stop the poor, panting, sweating horse. We halted the pretty and very frightened mare in her tracks. She was fully tacked and oddly had a piece of string hanging from her halter. Obviously, some knucklehead had tied up this mare with a piece of twine. There was only one way up or down to the beach and so we continued down, ponying the runaway horse on a spare lead rope behind us, knowing that we would inevitably meet the owner coming up on foot. Sure enough, there came a small party of riders including a duded-up cowboy with boots on the ground, embarrassed as all get out. Back at camp later, we joked about how easily we could have stolen that cute little mare.

Years later, when I had re-married and was living on my husband's fifty-five-acre grape ranch in Windsor, Nancy trailered her freckled white Arab, Woodrow—"Don't call him Woody, his name is Woodrow!", north on Hwy. 101 to ride with me. The ranch where I lived was surrounded by hundreds of acres of vineyards, which made for lovely riding in the soft soil. If we cut through the vineyards on horseback, it was just a short distance away from Riverfront Regional Park, which as its name implied, was scenically situated along the banks of the Russian River, winding around a picture-perfect lake. The park rules and regulations required visitors to stay within the park boundaries. But almost every day, making my own rules, I cut through the park and rode alone for miles along the river, often not arriving back home until dark.

The day she arrived with Woodrow in tow, happened to be in a wet winter month. Nancy and I rode through the muddy vineyards and over to the park, heading right out into the undesignated area. The soil in that area of the county is composed of heavy clay, which notoriously bogs down vehicles in the vineyards. Riding our horses, muddy to the knees, through a narrow, secluded draw near the river we began to hear the sounds of loud, high-pitched engines coming ever closer. Looking back, we saw a large pickup hurtling full speed ahead, quickly closing in on us. We were riding in a narrow area where there was no place to pull over and the banks were much too slippery to climb. Finding ourselves trapped, we simultaneously began to scream. The combination of our screaming and the deafening engine sounds of the pickups frightened the horses who are fight-or-flight animals. They quickly bolted in fear. Hearing a loud crash, we looked back again to see the oncoming truck, sliding into an embankment to avoid hitting us, with another truck behind it, crashing into the first truck. Attempting to stop our horses and thinking that we should go back to help, we heard the loud angry voices of the young men who were driving the trucks calling out to us, "We're going to kill you bitches!!!" The last thing I remember is, yelling to Nancy; "Let's get the hell outta here" and the two of us galloping full speed back to the safety of the park. It was one heck of a very muddy close call. Nancy likes to say that we've shared some "colorful experiences."

About the Author

Nancy J. Martin was born in San Francisco, raised in Marin County and migrated north to the Valley of the Moon, where she has resided since 1976.

Nancy & Milagro 2008

Also by Nancy J. Martin

Available at Amazon.com

www.ingramcontent.com/pod-product-compliance
Lightning Source LLC
Chambersburg PA
CBHW060330310726
48976CB00007B/2512